*One word,* Veritas was screaming at himself silently, trying to get through the unbearable waves of noise. *You've got to say one word! Only one word!*

Granny Hazelbide poked at him with the tip of one pointy black shoe, and was just getting ready to draw back her foot for an actual kick, when he finally succeeded in croaking out that word. It brought both old women to rigid attention as if it had been a Charm and a Spell and a Transformation all combined into one. The sound had come out of Veritas' mouth, strangled and deformed but comprehensible . . .

"Mules!"

"Mules," repeated the Grannys, looking at one another. "Do you suppose . . . ?"

*Berkley books by Suzette Haden Elgin*

## THE OZARK FANTASY TRILOGY

BOOK I: TWELVE FAIR KINGDOMS
BOOK II: THE GRAND JUBILEE
BOOK III: AND THEN THERE'LL BE FIREWORKS

# Suzette Haden Elgin

# And Then There'll Be Fireworks

## Book Three of the Ozark Fantasy Trilogy

BERKLEY BOOKS, NEW YORK

All of the characters in this book
are fictitious, and any resemblance
to actual persons, living or dead,
is purely coincidental.

This Berkley book contains the complete text
of the original hardcover edition.

AND THEN THERE'LL BE FIREWORKS

A Berkley Book / published by arrangement with Doubleday
& Company, Inc.

PRINTING HISTORY
Doubleday edition published 1981
Berkley edition / November 1983

ISBN: 0-425-06290-2

A BERKLEY BOOK ® TM 757,375
Berkley Books are published by The Berkley Publishing Group,
200 Madison Avenue, New York, New York 10016.
The name "BERKLEY" and the stylized "B" with design
are trademarks belonging to Berkley Publishing Corporation.
PRINTED IN THE UNITED STATES OF AMERICA

# And Then There'll Be Fireworks

# CHAPTER 1

The child struggled under his hands; and he blamed it
not at all. The sight of the Long Whip rising and falling
on the naked back of ten-year-old Avalon of Wommack
made his own stomach churn. Avalon was a slight and
scrawny child, narrow of shoulder, the copper Wommack hair gone dark now with the swift-pouring sweat
of her agony and clinging in a drenched coil along one
frail shoulder blade. Something about the nape of her
neck, where a babyish curl nestled all alone, tore at him
worse than the blood.

"Look you well," hissed Eustace Laddercane Traveller the 4th through clenched teeth, holding his
youngest son's head as every parent in Traveller Kingdom had learned it must be done. Not just the iron grip
that kept the small head from turning away, but the little finger of each hand jabbed cruelly into the corners of
the child's eyes, drawing the eyelids back taut against
any possible hint of their closing.

It hurt, of course; but not so much as the smack of
that Whip would hurt, should one of the College of
Deacons see the child avoiding its present duty: to
watch the public whipping of Avalon of Wommack.
And one day this boy he held so tightly now would per-
form the same service for the babe that swelled his

1

mother's belly this very moment, as his older children held their younger brothers and sisters all around him. His wife had not been spared, either, though Eustace Laddercane had requested it; her time was very near, and it a tenth child—this whipping was enough to set off her labor and see his tenth-born arrive in the public square. But the Tutor had been absolutely adamant about it. Should that happen, he'd told him, it would be a blessing for the newborn, its first sight in this world one guaranteed to further its moral education and set it on the straight path for life.

Should that happen, thought the father, he'd blind the babe with his own two thumbs before he'd let that be its first sight of the world . . . the Holy One grant that it *not* happen.

Avalon of Wommack was well shielded from any lustful eyes. The Whipping Cloth hung foursquare from its hooks above her head to her bare feet, with only the narrow space cut away at the back to allow the Whip room. But it did nothing to shield her screams. Eustace Laddercane hoped they hurt the ears of the Magicians of Rank that stood one at each corner of the cloth, twelve inches between them and their pitiful victim.

The whipping itself, now—no man could have done that, though not one had courage enough to stop it. It was Granny Leeward of Castle Traveller, her that was the own mother of the Castle Master, that wielded the Long Whip.

She'd explained Avalon of Wommack's grievous sins to them all carefully before she began the chastisement, looking all around her with those measuring eyes, counting. She knew precisely how many people should be there on the walkway that bordered the square, did the Granny. Ninety-one excused by the College of Deacons for illness near unto death, a sign of sure wickedness in those ninety and one; and seven hundred thirteen that left to be counted. Eustace Laddercane was certain that Granny Leeward was able to count each and every one of the seven hundred thirteen, and would have known if even one had been missing. They lined up by household and by height, the tallest at the back.

There still was not room for all of them within the Castle walls, and it had been necessary to lay out this whipping ground outside, burning away every last sprig and blade of growing life, grading it flat as the top of a table, anchoring down the board walkway that bordered it with spokes of ironwood hammered into chinks blasted out of the Tinaseeh rock. But that was changing. The people of Tinaseeh, they were dying with a terrifying speed, ten and twenty and more now in a single day . . . soon they'd be able to take their Whipping Cloth inside one of the courtyards, right into Roebuck . . . might could be soon they'd have ample space in the Castle Great Hall itself, and be hard put to it to find anybody left to whip.

Avalon of Wommack had sinned doubly. First she had sinned against the cause that bid the Chosen People of Tinaseeh repopulate this land, to replace the dying who by their very deaths had revealed the vileness of their souls. Avalon's father had brought her home a husband, a man of seventeen, and Avalon not only had not welcomed her bridegroom tenderly and obediently

3

as was expected of her, not only refused to go willingly
to the marriage bed where this male twice her size and
near twice her age might do her the favor of placing his
seed in her womb—Avalon had tried to hide herself
away. They had dragged her from a granary, half
suffocated already on the grain and on her terror. Despite the fact, Granny Leeward had hammered the point
home, that Avalon's womb had been through two full
cycles. And secondly, there was the additional fact that
Avalon of Wommack was a Two, and a female whose
name came to the numeral two was intended by destiny
to be passive and submissive and weak. The girl had also
sinned against her Naming.

That, the Granny had said, was the greater sin of the
two. A young girl, modest and timid as was fully appropriate, might be leniently treated for fearing the wed-
ding bed and the inevitable childbed that followed it.
She might well of had only a token stroke or two of the
Long Whip for that, provided she went then and did
her duty ever after.

But to rebel against her Naming was not just to rebel
against Jeremiah Thomas Traveller's orders to marry
and be fruitful, the orders of a mere man. It was rebel-
lion against the path laid out for her by the Holy One; a
fearsome evil, a defying of the divine law.

And so the number of lashes had been set at twice
twelve. A memorable number. Eustace Laddercane remembered only one other unfortunate to earn so high a
number as that, and that time it had been for stealing
food from the common stores and gorging on it. And

that time the Whip had fallen on the broad back of a man full grown.

The Long Whip whistled through the air—stroke seventeen. The Magicians of Rank put themselves to the trouble of calling out the number each time for the watchers, that they might not lose track and think that surely it had to be almost over.

At his side he felt a long shudder take his wife's body, and he dared a quick look, sure it was the birth pains, but she knew his thought as soon as he did, and without turning her head she murmured to him not to take foolish chances, that she was all right. All right, she said, but for the whipping.

Avalon of Wommack did not scream again after the nineteenth stroke, but Granny Leeward took care not to leave the people wondering what was the point of laying five more strokes on a body already dead.

"Praise be," said the Granny solemnly. "The household of this youngun can go tranquil to its beds this night. Avalon of Wommack has paid in full the debt of her wickedness, and she stands now in eternal bliss, smiling and singing at the right hand of the Holy One Almighty. Praise be!"

The Magicians of Rank raised their long shears as one man and cut the loops that held the Whipping Cloth to the hooks, and there was nothing then to see but a pile of bloody linen, very nearly flat, upon the stained ground.

Somebody's child, walking the edge of hysteria, screamed out over and over: "Where did Avalon of

Wommack go? *Where is she?*" And there was the ringing smack of a full blow across that child's face as its mother moved desperately to offer up a penalty before the College of Deacons could prescribe one.

And Granny Leeward's voice rose strong and sure—and why not, seeing as how she was little more than sixty and mighty young for a Granny—leading them in the hymn that had been chosen to end this particular whipping. It was seemly; its title was "Divine Pain, Willingly Endured." Except that Avalon of Wommack had not been willing.

The members of the College of Deacons moved along the walkway, their arms folded gravely over their chests, watching and listening for any sign of somebody singing with anything less than righteous enthusiasm. It was, after all, an occasion for celebration, what with Avalon of Wommack's eternal bliss and her family's tranquillity and all; and the College of Deacons was fully prepared to see to it that a suitable explanation was provided for anybody present that couldn't understand that on their own.

The little ones sang their hearts out, and the older ones sighed and released their grips upon the small heads just a mite. The children knew already; sing, sing loud, and sing joyful. Make a joyful noise . . . they knew. Or there'd be a smaller version of the Long Whip waiting at home, and the mother assigned a specific number of strokes to be laid on, by the Deacon that'd spotted the wavering voice. It made for hearty music.

Eustace Laddercane Traveller the 4th believed, really believed, in the Holy One Almighty. And there had not been a whipping yet that he had not raised his own voice in the closing hymn, almost roaring out the words, waiting for the divine wrath to reach the limit of Its endurance and strike Granny Leeward dead before his eyes. It had not happened yet, but his faith that it would was a rock on which he stood, and a comfort to him in the nights when often he dreamed it was a child of his loins that cringed and screamed and twisted under the strokes of the Whip.

"It went well, to my mind," said Nathan Overholt Traveller the 101st. "No faintings, no foolishness, and no punishments to pass out afterward—all very satisfactory."

The other three nodded, and agreed that it had gone well enough.

"Well enough, perhaps." That was Feebus Timothy Traveller the 6th, youngest of the Magicians of Rank on Tinaseeh. "But the child ought not to have died."

The two Farson brothers, Sheridan Pike the 25th and Luke Nathaniel the 19th, looked at each other. There were times when they wondered about Feebus Timothy, finding him a tad soft, wondering if there wasn't a slight taint of Airy blood there somewhere to account for what came near at times to romantic notions. Times when they felt he'd profit from a stroke or two of the Long Whip himself. He sorely needed toughening up.

"There is no room on Tinaseeh for a disobedient child," said Nathan Overholt harshly. "The subject is closed."

"There was a time," persisted Feebus Timothy,

7

"when we could have saved her, any one of us, no matter how many lashes she had taken."

"There was a time," said Sheridan Pike reasonably, "when we could cause the Mules to fly and carry us on their backs, and a time when the winds and the rains and the tides obeyed us. And that was that time, and it is gone. We deal now with *this* time."

The mention of the powers they had lost silenced them all. It was not something you got used to. Once you had been someone whose fingers could make a casual move or two and a cancer would shrivel and disappear inside the sick one's body, leaving no trace behind. Once you had been someone that could SNAP through space, moving from the Wilderness Lands of Tinaseeh, across the vastness of the Oceans of Remembrances and of Storms, to land less than a second later in the courtyard of any of the twelve Castles of the planet Ozark. Once you had been someone who saw to it that the rain fell only when and where it was needed, and that the harvests were always bountiful, and that the snow fell only deep enough and often enough to be an amusement for the children and a change for their elders . . . once.

Now, on the other hand, it was as Sheridan Pike had said. Now they had to deal with *this* time. Four Magicians of Rank, their titles as hollow as their stomachs and their gaunt faces, garbed in a black grown shiny with wear, and their only power now the power of fear. It was a painful comedown, for they had been truly mighty.

Luke Nathaniel Farson had been picking idly at his

front teeth with his thumbnail, a maddening little noise in the silence; and then he stopped, just before they could demand for him to, and asked: "Do you suppose it's true, that rumor about the Yallerhounds?"

"Luke Nathaniel!" Even Feebus Timothy got in on the outrage.

"I don't know," mused the other man. "They're hungry. We're hungry, here at the Castle . . . think of the people in the town. A Yallerhound, or a giant cavecat, that's a sizable quantity of meat. And though it's true I can't think of any of the men with strength enough left to take a cavecat, you know as well as I do that a boy of three could catch a Yallerhound. All you have to do is call the creature, and it will come to you."

"Nobody," said Sheridan Pike, "nobody at *all*, would eat a Yallerhound. They would starve first."

"They will, then," said Luke Nathaniel. "Those that haven't already."

"Change the subject," ordered Sheridan Pike flatly. "Can't any of you think of *something* that's not intolerable to talk about? You've lost your magic powers, but I wasn't aware that you'd lost your minds as well."

"Well," said Feebus Timothy, "we could discuss today's scheduled urgent and significant meeting. That's not intolerable, just useless, and silly, and stupid."

"Your sarcasm is very little help, Cousin," said Sheridan Pike.

"All right, then, I'll ask seriously. What *is* on today's agenda?"

"A discussion of the situation."

"Again?" Feebus Timothy was serious now, serious

and flabbergasted. "Whatever for? We have had nine hundred and ninety-nine 'discussions of the situation' and we have yet to arrive at a single—"

Sheridan Pike cut him off. "Jeremiah Thomas Traveller is Master of this Castle, master of the four of us, son of Granny Leeward, and representative of the Holy One upon this earth. If he says we are to discuss the situation yet one more time—or one hundred more times —then we will discuss it."

Feebus Timothy snorted. "The only thing in all that that impresses *me*, Cousin, is the claim that he's Leeward's son. *That* I believe, it being a matter of record; and *that* I'm impressed by. As for the rest of it . . . if you'll pardon a phrase from the formspeech . . . cowflop."

"You talk a good line," said Luke Nathaniel Farson. "But I have yet to see you do more than talk."

Sheridan Pike moved smoothly to cover the charged silence, and observed that another discussion was not necessarily a waste of time.

"Each time we meet," he said, "there is the possibility that we will hit upon something we have overlooked before, colleagues. Somewhere there is a clue to be found, if only we were wise enough to spot it."

"The clue you seek," retorted Feebus Timothy, "lies in pseudocoma on a narrow bed at Castle Brightwater. Where we put her, we wise Magicians of Rank, these sixteen months past."

"Nonsense!"

"Not nonsense," said Nathan Overholt, knowing he plowed ground already furrowed to exhaustion, but too tired to care, "not nonsense at all. Feebus Timothy is somewhat confused, and somewhat overdramatic, but the facts of the matter are obvious. While Responsible of Brightwater went about her interfering and infuriating business on this planet, we were truly Magicians, with the power of Formalisms & Transformations at our command. From the moment we laid her in pseudo-coma on that bed my cousin refers to so poetically, our power began to wane . . . and now it is gone. Entirely, completely, wholly gone. *Magic* is gone . . . and on Tinaseeh we have no science. The question is: *why?*"

"We have no science because we never needed it," said Sheridan Pike disgustedly. "Magic was a great deal faster than science ever hoped to be, and far more efficient."

"No, no . . . that was not my question! And you know it, don't you?"

"Of course I know it!"

"Then stop playing the fool!"

"He is not playing the fool," said Luke Nathaniel wearily, "he is just cross, like the rest of us. And we have considered that question so many times already."

"Magic," said Nathan Overholt, "is a great web, a great web in always changing equilibrium. Touch it anywhere, change it anyhow, and you affect the whole. When we removed Responsible of Brightwater from that web—"

"We haven't removed her. She's in better health than any of us. In pseudocoma you don't *need* to eat."

"In a sense," Nathan Overholt went on, "we removed her. We changed her from an active principle to a passive one . . . and yet she is a female. How can a female represent an active principle?"

"Granny Leeward is exceedingly 'active' with the Long Whip," observed Luke Nathaniel. "And she is female."

"She is not a *principle*—she is only an item."

Feebus Timothy longed to lay his head, still aching from the screams of Avalon of Wommack, down on the table, right then and there, and go to sleep. They had been over it. And over it. The difference between an item and a principle. The difference between substitution of a null term and substitution of a specified term. The degree of shift in an equation sufficient to destroy its reversibility—or restore it. And over and over . . . what role had Responsible of Brightwater, a girl of fifteen like any other girl of fifteen to the eye, played in that equation, such that the cancellation of *her* input had been enough to destroy the entire system?

There were never any answers. That she had known a little magic, some of it more advanced than was suitable for a female or even legal, they all knew. The four of them had been present when Responsible fell into Granny Leeward's trap and changed the old woman's black fan into a handful of rotting jet-black mushrooms before their astonished eyes. Jeremiah Thomas Traveller had been mightily impressed by that, as the Granny had intended him to be.

But *they* were Magicians of Rank. It was a Transformation, certainly, and the girl should not have been able to do it, but it was trivial. It was a baby trick, such as any one of them might have done—in a less ugly way

—to entertain guests at a celebration of some kind. It was probable that it had been as much blind luck as skill, and mostly the product of the girl's rage; for she had lain in torment while they watched her and mocked her misery, suffering from the gift of Anderson's Disease, the deathdance fever that Granny Leeward had ordered them to impose as punishment for her scandalous behavior. And she'd shown no sign of any talent for things magical but that one . . . nor had she been able to stand against them when the nine Magicians of Rank had chosen to impose pseudocoma upon her or during the months that had dragged by since. If there was something special about her, why had she not leaped up from that bed and laughed at them and put all of *them* into pseudocoma?

It was hopeless.

"It's hopeless," he said aloud. "Hopeless."

The others looked at him, suddenly caught by the nuance of his voice. He was young, and he was inexperienced, but he had been a skilled Magician of Rank. Now they detected something . . . a note of petulance. Petulance?

Nathan Overholt Traveller reached over abruptly and laid his hand on the younger man's forehead and swore a broad word.

"He's burning up with fever!" he said. "One of you get the Granny, and tell her to lose no time coming down here!"

It had been bound to happen sooner or later. Sickness, the Master of this Castle had been telling everyone, sickness and death, were nothing more than the

13

marks of wickedness and sin made visible in the flesh. Only the Holy One culling the rotten fruit from the crop and leaving the sound and the wholesome behind. It made an entertaining sermon, and perhaps dulled grief for some . . . after all, if those that suffered and died deserved their fate, then what was there to grieve over?

But the Magicians of Rank had been uneasy, listening. For if one of them, one of the Magicians of Rank, one of the Family, were to fall sick or, the Twelve Gates forbid, to die—how was that to be explained? The urgency of preventing that had provided them with a shaky justification for the extra rations they shared in secret in the Castle, while tadlings cried with hunger in the houses of the town. *Eggs*, they had been eating . . . it was safe to assume that no one else on Tinaseeh had seen an egg in six months or more, much less eaten one. And now this? It must not happen.

"Why call the Granny?" demanded one of the others, and Nathan Overholt took time from rubbing the temples of his brother's head to give him a look of contempt.

"We have no magic now, you benastied fool," he spat, beside himself with worry, and his elegant manners and speech forgotten for once, "and no medicine either. We have *nothing*—except what the Grannys know. The ancient simples. The herbs and teas and potions and plasters of the times *before* magic, the Holy One have mercy on us all! Now *get* her!"

"Nathan Overholt—"

"You think," shouted Nathan, "you think that if one

14

of us falls to a fever we will be able to stand on the whipping ground and convince the people of Tinaseeh that we order that Whip laid on out of our own innocence of all sin? You think that Granny Leeward would scruple to set that Long Whip to your back, or to mine, if that seemed necessary to further the cause of the Chosen People? Dozens, man, don't you realize that if Feebus Timothy has it we may *all* be in the same fix, whatever it is—and it could be *anything?* Now go!"

He went around behind his brother and clasped the young man's head in his hands, closing his eyes, concentrating fiercely. It was an act he knew to be only superstition. But perhaps. Perhaps there was still some fragment of healing in it. He could not do nothing at all. He had no desire to die like Avalon of Wommack had died; nor did he want to learn how many strokes of the Long Whip it would take to kill a strong man in reasonably good condition.

15

# CHAPTER 2

Mount Troublesome was not much, as mountains go; it peaked at a tad past four thousand feet, and it hadn't a glacier or a crevasse to its name. On the other hand, though it didn't live up to the "Mount" part, it more than made up for that in its fidelity to the "Troublesome" part. It missed no smallest opportunity for ravines to get stuck in and caves to get lost in and vast thickets to be scratched ragged in; and it was abundantly generous in poisonous ivies and creepers winding along the ground and up around the trees to hang down and smack you in the face. Springs were everywhere, trickling along under matted undergrowth that looked solid as a stable roof, till you set foot on it and sank in icy water up to your knees. There were waterfalls enough to go around, pretty white water gushing over sheer rock faces into pools circled by ferns and near-willows. The pools were tempting to the eye, and might of been pleasant-feeling, but you waded them at your peril and the pleasure of dozens of small ferocious yellow snakes with ingeniously notched teeth. It did happen to be a fact that Mount Troublesome was the tallest thing on the entire continent of Marktwain.

The seven old women toiling their way up its tangled sides were more than satisfied with the obstacles it presented. If it had been any worse, there was considerable doubt in their minds that they could of made it to the top at all.

"Drat the ornery female!" Granny Sherryjake had declared after the second time a whole hour had to be wasted finding a way round a berry thicket as impenetrable as solid rock and twice as unpleasant. And she went on to expand on that, and elaborate on it, and weave variations on it, as the hours went by and it became obvious that there was no way they could reach the top before nightfall. They'd be overnighting out on the mountain.

But Granny Hazelbide, that was in residence along with Granny Gableframe at Castle Brightwater, had taken exception to that. It was *fully* appropriate, she'd said, slapping back at a branch that had slapped her first, for a woman named Troublesome to choose a mountain named Troublesome when she went into exile.

"Fully appropriate, and seemly," said Granny Hazelbide. "I'd of done the same exact thing, in her place."

"Well," grumbled Sherryjake, "there may be something to what you say."

"I should hope and declare there is. Naming is *naming!*"

"But," went on the other doggedly, "I do *not* see that there was any special merit to be gained from her establishing herself at the very most tip *top* of this accursed hump of dirt and rock. She was not named *Peak* of Troublesome, you know. Halfway up would of done it, seems to me. Quarterways up."

"Troublesome of Brightwater was instructed to take herself as far away from the rest of the population of Brightwater as it was possible for her to get," said Granny Frostfall firmly. "I hold with Hazelbide; she did what was proper. But I surely do not find that it makes for a pleasant little stroll."

"Time was," fussed Granny Gableframe, "this would of been no more than that, for any of us."

"And in such a time," snorted Granny Frostfall, "we'd none of us of crossed a city *street* to pay a call on Troublesome of Brightwater. Can't say as how I see that it applies, Gableframe."

Granny Gableframe didn't bother to argue, but sighed a long sigh and took a firmer grip on her walking stick with her thin old fingers. It wouldn't do to lose it.

Grannys had always been thin, that went with the territory; but these seven were thin to the bone, and those bones pained them. Grannys had always been old; but up till recently they'd been protected from the usual miseries of old age by their own Granny Magic, and from its more *un*usual miseries by the skills of the Magicians and the Magicians of Rank. Without that protection, things had changed for them. Angina and arthritis, gall-bladder colic and kidney trouble, ulcers and headaches and high blood pressure, all the bodily discomforts taken for granted as the lot of any aged woman on Old Earth, had struck the Grannys of Ozark. It was even said that at Castle Clark—though she denied it fiercely—Granny Golightly was developing a cataract in her right eye.

Under the circumstances, when Granny Gableframe

19

first proposed that the seven of them should go up to
the mountaintop and talk to Troublesome of Brightwater, the hilarity had been like a squawkercoop with a
serpent inside, and two servingmaids had come running
to find out what the commotion was.

"You are daft, Gableframe," the other Grannys had
said with a single voice, and they'd sat in their rockers
and cackled and held their aching sides at the very idea.
Seven creaking old ladies, half blind and half deaf, feet
too swollen to go in their shoes and bones so brittle they
barely dared move them—and they were to trek up the
meanest mountain on Marktwain in the middle of the
autumn? It was a fool idea to top all fool ideas.

"That does take the rag off the bush, Gableframe,"
they'd said, and it was unanimous.

"And what *do* you propose to do, ladies?" Gableframe had challenged them, standing there arms akimbo
and her sharp chin stuck out ahead of her. "You propose to just sit here, do you? While the crops all die and
the animals sicken and the people do the same, and Responsible of Brightwater lies month after weary month
on that white counterpane, so still the only reason I can
believe she's alive is that her body has yet to *mortify?*
Well, ladies? You laugh right prompt, real quick to
make fun, *you* are! But I don't hear you offering any
plans of your own."

They did know two things, there was that. In the first
months after Responsible had been struck down, while
the power of magic was waning but not yet exhausted,
the Grannys had managed to learn two small pieces of
information. They'd read tea leaves, they'd swung their

golden rings on long black threads, they'd stared into springwater till their eyes were red and weeping, night after night. And back at them had come two scraps.

The reason behind the trouble, the reason behind Responsible's deathlike interminable sleep, was "an important man." That had come first, and after much labor, and had irritated them considerably. Then there had been the search for that man's location in this world, holding the golden rings over the maps, holding their breaths as well, waiting for one ring to begin its telltale swinging and circling. All atremble like they were, it took a sharp eye to tell when the movement was of its own self and when it was just the doings of a Granny that's hand was no longer steady.

And then there'd been argument. The Spells were so little use by then, the movement of the rings so near no movement at all, and so ambiguous—was it Tinaseeh or was it Kintucky? All of a week they'd nattered over that, half for one and half for the other, knowing that if they made the wrong choice there'd be no second chance. There weren't resources enough for trying twice, for one thing. And for another, if anything was to be done it had to be done swiftly; there was nothing in the way of extra resources of *time*, either.

Grannys Gableframe, Whiffletree, and Edging had been strong for Tinaseeh, swearing it was Jeremiah Thomas Traveller that was the "important man." Did he not, after all, rule that continent with a fist of iron, and hadn't he always? And hadn't he always hated Responsible of Brightwater and everything she stood for?

"Hmmph," said Granny Cobbledrayke of Castle

McDaniels, "it's not Jeremiah Thomas as rules Tina-seeh, it's his mother, her that took Leeward as her Granny Name and is about as much like a leeward side in a storm as a lizard's like a bellybutton. Don't give *me* Jeremiah Thomas Traveller for an 'important man'—he's a mama's boy, and always was."

She, and the rest of the Marktwain Grannys, had been set on Kintucky, and Castle Wommack. Hadn't Responsible herself, they argued, run away from Castle Wommack—her that wasn't afraid of anything living or dead—run *away*, rather than face Lewis Motley Wommack? And wasn't it Lewis Motley Wommack that now governed all of Kintucky?

"He is barely twenty-one years old . . . *wouldn't* be, not quite yet," Gableframe protested. "A *boy* yet, last time we saw him! Here for the Jubilee, remember? With his little sister Jewel set to tag around after him and keep him out of mischief? How can that one be the 'important man,' I ask you?"

"He is important on Kintucky," said Sherryjake.

"Well, we don't know how that came to be," grumbled the others. "We don't know atall. Way our magic was working in those last months, for all we know the messages we got were plain scrambled . . . might could be Jacob Donahue Wommack the 23rd's still hale and hearty and Master of that Castle and the whole tale about it being Lewis Motley in charge is no more than a puckerwrinkle in a puny Spell. Who'd be fool enough to put a wild colt like that one in charge of a Kingdom? Now I *ask* you . . ."

But the time had come when the decision had to be

made; and for want of anything better to base it on they'd deferred to Granny Hazelbide, seeing as it was Hazelbide had had the raising of Responsible of Brightwater and knew her best of any of them.

Now, fighting the thorns and the vines and the poison weeds, keeping a sharp eye for the false earth over running water, making a hardscrabble way up through a drizzle that threatened to be a rain and praying they'd find at least an overhang to shelter them through this night, they hoped they'd decided rightly. Everything rode on this one throw of the dice, and Granny Hazelbide shivered with more than the fever that plagued her now every day of her life, thinking what she'd done if it was the wrong choice and she had convinced the others of it. And what they'd do to her . . . law, *that* would be a production!

"Ah, Hazelbide," said Granny Willowithe, her that almost never spoke, and had done her grannying in the farther reaches of the Kingdom where there were few to bother her, "if you are *wrong!*" It was always that way. Those as spoke rarely, when they did speak it tended to be significant and to be what everybody else was thinking and hadn't gotten up gumption to give voice to.

Troublesome of Brightwater woke to a wind howling round her cabin doors and windows, and that was ordinary enough. She woke also to a downright infuriated rapping on her cabin door, and that was distinctly *not* ordinary. Over ten years she'd been here now, and she'd never had a visitor but her little sister, and that only three times. It could not be her little sister this time.

She listened again, and stretched in the warmth of her bed, wondering if it had been maybe something blown by the winds, or something in a dream, half a mind to go back to sleep. And then the hollering came: "Troublesome of Brightwater, *will* you open this door? Or have you taken to murdering old ladies along with the rest of your wicked ways?"

That brought her up out of her bed in a hurry. Old ladies, was it, on her doorsill? She went to the door just as she was, and stood there before them mothernaked and barefoot, with no cover but the heavy black hair that tumbled almost to her knees. She held the door with one hand and set the other on the curve of her shameless hip, and she sighed a sigh of sheer wonderment.

"Whatever in all the world?" breathed Troublesome of Brightwater, looking them over. "Whatever in all the wondering twelvesquare world?"

The Grannys were a sight to behold, for sure. They were wet and they were dirty and they were nettle-stung, and they were cold and wrinkled and miserable. With no more Housekeeping Spells to use, and nothing around for a tidy-up but one stream the width of their hand trickling over slabs of bare rock, they were as pitiful a representation of seven old ladies as had ever met the eye.

"Out of my way, trollop," announced Granny Gableframe, and would of pushed right past Troublesome into the welcome warmth of the cabin; but the young woman barred her way with one sturdy arm.

"I'm no trollop, Granny Gableframe," she said. "I'm virgin as I came from my mother's womb—and that's

24

more than any one of you here can say back at me, as I recollect. As for my costume, I don't recall sending out any invitations. You've gotten potluck, Grannys."

"Law, the creature's enjoying it," muttered Granny Hazelbide. She'd had the raising of *her*, too. "Troublesome," she demanded, "will you for the love of decency drop that arm and let us in? We are tired near to death, we spent all yesterday on this mountain and all last night in a cave full of varmints and dripping water, and we've no magic any more to ease the toll all that has taken. Would it pleasure you to see one of us drop dead right here before your eyes, you dreadful female?"

Troublesome dropped her arm at that and let them by, saying: "Well, that's more fair. A trollop I'm not, but a dreadful female I'm willing to admit to. Do come in, and I'll put the kettle on and stir up the fire. I don't suppose youall'd take your clothes off and let me hang them to dry, would you?"

That met the frigid silence she'd anticipated, and she nodded her head in resignation.

"Stay cold and wet, then," she said, "and die of pneumonia, not on my doorstep but on my hearthstone—but don't you lay it to my account. There's not a one of you as has anything different to her body than I have myself, and I do believe I could bear the sight of your old skinny-skin-skins . . . for sure I would not lust after you! But if you rank your modesty higher than your misery, so be it; I'll not squabble with you."

The cabin was small and bare, and even after Troublesome got the fire crackling in the fireplace the best she could do was pull up a rough board bench with no back to it for them all to sit on and try to bake the damp from their bones. Troublesome had no rugs, and no curtains; her bed was a pallet laid on a rope frame in the corner, she had one straight chair and one rocker and one low stepladder and a small square table and a cookstove. And except for a bucket or two and a shelf here and there, that was it. The Grannys were bemused by it, even with their teeth chattering.

"Don't have eight cups, do you?" asked Granny Sherryjake.

Troublesome chuckled, and admitted she didn't, and served them up the scalding tea in an assortment of jars and ladles and whatnots that was ingenious, but not elegant.

"Never needed more than three before," she told them. "One to drink with, one to measure with, and one in the dishpan soaking."

"I can't say as you exactly . . . do yourself *proud*," commented Granny Frostfall, and a kind of snort of agreement ran down the bench.

"No, I don't suppose I do," Troublesome agreed.

"Tain't natural," said one, and Troublesome's eyebrows rose.

"You expected things up here to be natural?" she asked.

The Grannys sighed all together, seeing it was a hopeless case, and Troublesome went to a row of three pegs on a wall by her bed and took down a long dress all in a soft scarlet wool and slipped it over her head.

"There," she said, "now I'll not be quite such an offense to your eyes." And her long fingers were almost

26

too quick for those same fourteen sharp eyes to see as she put the mass of hair into a braid and wound it up around her head and fastened it tight.

It was unjust that anything so wicked should be so beautiful, or so clever, or so serene, or so happy with her lot—especially the last—and the Grannys stared glumly into the fire and pondered on that.

"Well, ladies," Troublesome said at last, sitting herself down on an upended bucket with her arms wrapped round her knees, since it wouldn't of been mannerly to take a chair while the old women huddled on that bench, "now you're a bit warmer and dryer, maybe you'd tell me what I'm beholden to for the pleasure of your company?"

"Maybe you might offer us a bite of breakfast first!" snapped Granny Gableframe. "*If* you care to spare it!"

"It's already cooking," said Troublesome calmly, "but I can't do anything much to hurry it along. And while we're waiting on it—no, I don't have eight plates either, but as it happens I *do* have eight spoons—while we're waiting on it I see no reason not to make the time go by speaking up on the reason for this visit. I'm afraid I'm not much for visitors."

The Grannys allowed as how they never *would* of figured that out if she hadn't mentioned it, and she chuckled again.

"Earn your keep, you dear old things," she teased them, brazen as brazen, "earn your keep. What brings you hanging round my door all unannounced and unkempt, with snow before the week's out or my name's not Troublesome of Brightwater? You should be home, each in your rocker with your knitting, by your own fire, telling terrible stories to the tadlings."

Granny Hazelbide was embarrassed; true, this one was properly Named, and her outrageousness came as no surprise to anybody, but it *had* been her, poor Granny Hazelbide, that had tried to keep some control over her when she was a little girl at Castle Brightwater.

"Troublesome," she said sadly, "have you no feelings atall?"

"Probably not," said Troublesome promptly. "Feelings about what?"

"Times are *hard*, young woman," said Hazelbide, "times are fearsome hard! You talk of sitting by our fires . . . there's precious little left to lay a fire *with*, down in the towns. People are suffering, and your own sister lies near death in the Castle. How can you sit there and face us and make jokes over it all?"

"Would it help," Troublesome put the question, "if I moaned about it instead? Would it ease anybody's fever, stop anybody's bleeding, or put food in anybody's stomach or fire on their hearth? Would it wake my sister —who is *not*, by the way, anywhere near death. Not as near as the seven of you, I assure you."

"Ah, you're heartless," Granny Hazelbide mourned. "Just heartless!"

Troublesome said nothing at all, but waited and watched, and they began to smell the porridge on the stove and their stomachs knotted.

"Well, we want you to make a journey," said Granny Gableframe when it finally became clear that they'd get no more out of the girl. "A long and a perilous journey. And that's why we're here . . . to ask you. Politely."

Troublesome stared at her, black brows knit over her nose, and gave a sharp "tchh" with her tongue.

"A journey? Go on a trip?"

"Yes. And a good long one."

She stood up and went to the stove and began passing the porridge over to them, warning them to use their shawls to hold on so they'd not burn their fingers.

"Certainly can't hurt the shawls, the state *they're* in," she said.

She watched them while they ate; and seeing that they were truly hungry, she didn't bother them, but busied herself pouring more tea and serving more porridge until it seemed to her that everybody was at last satisfied and she could gather up the motley collection of serving things in her apron and put it all into a pan of hot soapy water.

Whereupon she sat down, shaking her hands to dry them, and said, "No more excuses, now. You're dry, and you're warm, and you're fed and watered. It's too cold for you to be taking baths at your age, so you'll have to stay dirty, and I've no remedies for your other miseries; I've made you as comfortable as I'm capable of. Now I'll have you tell. me about this journey, thank you kindly."

"We want you to go to Castle Wommack," said Granny Hazelbide, and Troublesome almost fell off her makeshift stool in astonishment.

"To Kintucky? Granny, you've lost your mind entirely! However would I get to Castle Wommack?"

"On a ship."

"Granny Hazelbide, there's no ship goes to Kintucky any more, and no supplies to last the journey if there were. You've been nibbling something best left on its stem, *I* say."

"We have a ship," said Hazelbide, putting one stubborn word after another, "and a crew—not much of a crew, but it'll serve in this instance—and supplies enough to get all of you to Kintucky and back. Including the Mule you'll be taking along to get you from the coast to the Castle."

"Dozens!" said Troublesome. "I'd of said that was impossible."

"It wasn't cheap."

"It took all we had," put in Granny Whiffletree, "and all that the Grannys had on Oklahomah, and a contribution or two—not necessarily voluntary, if you take my meaning—from a few useless Magicians and Magicians of Rank. But we did it."

"Bribed the ship captain, did you? And bribed the crew?"

"That we did."

"And you think they'll stay bribed!"

"We do. The captain's a Brightwater, and all but one of the crew as well. And that one's a McDaniels. They'll stay bribed."

"Supposing," hazarded Troublesome, leaning forward, "that I was such a lunatic as to go gallivanting off to Kintucky in the middle of the autumn . . . just suppose that, *which* I'm not . . . what precisely is my goal, other than to drown myself and the captain and the crew and that poor Mule?"

They told her, and they watched her face go thoughtful, and Granny Gableframe pinched the next Granny down on the bench, gently; they knew then that they had her.

"I agree," said Troublesome slowly, "that it's sure to be Lewis Motley Wommack the 33rd. I do agree on that. Not a thing Jeremiah Thomas Traveller could have done that would account for what's happened, but that Wommack boy is something else again, and I do believe he lay with Responsible while the Jubilee was going on."

"So *that's* who it was!" exclaimed Granny Hazelbide. "How did you know?"

"Ask me no questions, Granny, I'll tell you no lies," said Troublesome. "It makes no nevermind how I knew. But you've chosen right, for sure and for certain. However . . . you've nothing here but missing pieces."

"Explain yourself!"

"*Did* you learn, before your magic wound down, that if somebody went to see this 'important man' it would make some difference in the course of events on Ozark?" Troublesome stared them down, and they had to admit that they hadn't.

"And *did* you learn that just because he's the cause of Responsible's hearty nap he knows how to wake her up again?

"And *did* you learn that even if my sister *was* awake again, she'd be able to do something about all this tribulation we suffer from? Did you?"

It was no to both, of course, and they had to admit it.

31

"But you'd send me half round the world on a wild goose chase, on the slim tagtail of a chance that there *might* be some use to it?"

And they agreed that they would.

"Well," said Troublesome. "I never heard such nonsense."

"Sass!"

"No, I never did. Unless it was youall coming up here like you did, risking pneumonia coming up and breaking every bone in your bodies going down—'cause you pay me mind, now, if you thought you had a hard time getting up here, you just wait till you try getting back down! It's a heap faster, but it's not a safe trip. No way, no way in this world, am I going to take any part in such a fool project, and you should of known better than to ask me."

"Your sister lies—"

"Tell me no more about how my sister lies!" shouted Troublesome. "And tell me no more about the suffering of the people down there below! Wasn't it those very same people that would not *heed* my sister when she tried to warn them, and voted away the government that was holding them all together? Wasn't it?"

"Troublesome—"

"And for all my sister had done for them, was it not those very same people that showed her no more gratitude than they would a stick? That's the people we're talking about, amn't I right, Grannys? Don't you ask me to feel sorry for those people—I despise them for a pack of contemptible ignorant two-faced good-for-nothing belly-creeping *serpents*, do you hear me? If their stomachs hurt them and their backs pain them and their hearts are broken, they've asked for that, and no call to come whimpering to me! They made their beds, let them wallow in them and cry in their pillows."

"And your sister?" said Granny Hazelbide, ever so carefully, in the hush. When Troublesome got going, she gave a spectacular performance, and even the Grannys were impressed just a tad.

"It is well known," said Troublesome of Brightwater in tones of ice, "that I have no natural human feelings. My sister can rot there for all I care—not that she will, that doesn't go with it, but she's *welcome* to—and you know it perfectly well. Ask any man, woman, or tadling on Marktwain about the compassion and the warm heart of Troublesome of Brightwater and see what you get back, if you don't know it already!"

Troublesome wasn't out of breath, but she was out of patience and way beyond out of hospitality. She stood up then and ordered them off, ignoring what they said about needing to rest, stuffing a careless handful of peachapples in a sack with some cold biscuits and shoving it at them for food on the journey home, telling them where the water was safe to drink and which paths to stay shut of. Warning them of a place where the snakes were thick this time of year because of a rock that got warm each day in the sun, and all but slamming her door behind them. They were back out in the weather and the downhill trek ahead of them before they could catch their breaths, and they heard the thump of that bucket as it hit the wall when she gave it a toss across the room.

"Well!" said Granny Frostfall. "I've seen manners, and I've seen manners . . . but she does beat all. She is every last thing she's made out to be, and some left over, and I'll wager she eats nails for breakfast when she's got no company to see her."

"She has a reputation to maintain," pointed out Granny Hazelbide.

"What's important," said Granny Gableframe, "and all that matters now except for getting down this dratted mountain, is that she'll do it."

"We're sure of that, Gableframe? I don't see it!"

"Oh, we're sure," said Gableframe; and Granny Hazelbide and Granny Sherryjake agreed. "We had her the minute she asked us to tell her about it, don't you know anything atall? If she'd turned us a deaf ear, now, and refused to even listen, and sent us all packing without so much as letting us tell her why we were here . . . well, that would of been Troublesome's way."

"Oh, yes," said Granny Hazelbide. "We've got her fast, the Twelve Corners preserve us all."

"But how'll she know where to go? How to find the ship?"

"I had that all on a slip of paper before ever we started up this overblown hill," sniffed Granny Hazelbide. "And tucked away safe in the pocket of my skirt. And it's tucked away safe now in her own hand, everything she needs to know. She gave that bucket quite a fling, there at the last, and she may well pitch the bench we sat on into her fire—but she'll keep that piece of paper safe. Every last *detail* she needs to know, it's on there."

"Law, Granny Hazelbide," said one or two. And "My stars, Hazelbide."

"Well, I know her," said the Granny. "I know her well."

"Can't say as I envy you that."

"I don't envy my *self* that, but there's times it's useful," said Granny Hazelbide. "And now let's us head for home. Might could be we'll make it before dark. Like Troublesome said, it's a sight faster going down than coming up."

# CHAPTER 3

*Smalltrack* was neither a supply freighter nor a pleasure craft. The smell aboard, in spite of a powerful scrubbing, made you instantly aware that it had been a fishing boat for a very long time. Having the Mule aboard didn't improve matters, since Dross had no respect whatsoever for a human being's ideas about waste disposal; she added a new fragrance to the prevailing reek of blood and entrails and ancient slime. The captain and the four men of his crew had been on workboats of one kind or another all their lives; if they noticed the smell atall, they paid it little mind. They knew themselves fortunate that it was wintry weather, and no hot sun broiling down to bring everything to a constant simmer and perk. As for their passenger, if she found conditions not to her liking, they didn't mind that atall.

If pushed, all five would have acknowledged a relish for the idea that Troublesome of Brightwater might not be all that comfortable crossing the Ocean of Storms to Kintucky in their racketydrag old boat. They didn't precisely want her to suffer, being good-natured men, but they were in mutual accord that she had a trifle discomfort coming to her. If the mechanisms of the universe saw fit to provide that discomfort without any call for their hands meddling in it, why, they found that positively Providential. It spoke to their sense of the fitness of things.

They were Marktwainers—four, including the captain, being Brightwaters by birth, and a single McDaniels finishing up the party—and they were conscious enough that the woman who spent her time silent on an upturned barrel in the stern, looking out over the rough water, was their kinswoman. It comforted Gabriel John McDaniels the 21st that he was just a tad less related to her than the other four, but they all recognized it as a burden to be borne. Relations, like poison plants and balky Mules and the occasional foolfish spoiling a catch, were part of the territory; wasn't anybody didn't have kinfolk they'd just as soon *not* of.

They'd had their instructions from the Grannys: "You leave her alone, she'll leave you alone." Same instructions as for most pesky and viperous things in this world, and they'd proved accurate enough. She sat there on her barrel by the hour, peering through hooded eyes they none of them would of cared to look into directly. If she wanted a drink of water, or something to eat, or a blanket to wrap round her strong thin shoulders, she got it without bothering any of them. If there was anything she wanted that she didn't have—and likely there was, though it was said she lived a spare and scrimped existence on her lonely mountaintop—she didn't mention it. And if a line fouled near to her, or a solar collector was wrong in its tilt, she fixed whatever was awry, without fuss and without error and with no assistance from the crew.

38

"Uncanny, she is," muttered Haven McDaniels Brightwater the 4th, some six hours out to sea. "Just *uncanny!*" He cleared his throat and stared up at the gray flat lid of the sky as if he was indifferent to the whole thing, just mentioning it in passing. "Can't say as how I wouldn't rather of had something else along . . . say a serpent, or maybe a Yallerhound."

Gabriel John McDaniels spat over the side to signify his disgust and demanded to know what Haven McDaniels had come *along* for, if that was the way he felt about it.

"What'd you expect?" he asked, jamming his hands into his pockets and setting his feet wide against the roll of the boat. "You expect a fine lady sitting on a tusset? With needlework to her hand, maybe, and a kerchief to her delicate little nose? That is Troublesome of Brightwater back there, just as agreed upon with the Grannys, and exactly as advertised."

"I know it," said Haven McDaniels sullenly. "You think I don't know it?"

"Well, then," Gabriel John answered him, "there's no call to comment on it. I strongly misdoubt the Grannys would of offered each of us the sum they did if we'd been taking a Yallerhound to Kintucky. We're being paid for the hazard of the thing . . . and she's rightly named, is Troublesome! Rightly named, her as could fry your heart in your chest with no more'n her two blue eyes, if she'd a mind to."

The captain heard that, and it didn't surprise him. He'd heard the rest, too, but he'd been ignoring it. One of the advantages to captaining so small a boat was that neither crew nor anybody else aboard could keep anything from him. He spoke up sharp and quick.

"That's enough of that, Gabriel John McDaniels," he rapped out. "*Days* we've got ahead of us, this trip. Bad weather and poor food and none of us truly fit . . . last thing we need here is superstitious claptrap fouling the air."

"Now, Captain—"

"I said it was *enough*. You hear me? I can speak louder, should there be call for to do so. You look to the weather, Gabriel John, and to this leaky woodbucket we travel in so precariously, and leave the tall tales to the tadlings and the Grannys. I'm purely astonished, hearing such stuff from a full-grown man, and him with four years' full service now on the water."

Gabriel John McDaniels was not impressed, and he was not about to drop his eyes to the captain. He'd not spent his own childhood roaming the Wilderness Lands of Marktwain with the man, but his *daddy* had; and many a night he'd seen the two of them with more whiskey in them than had pleased his mother. He held Captain Adam Sheridan Brightwater the 73rd in no awe.

"You're obliged to take that stand," he said, speaking right up. "We know that, all of us. But there on that nailbarrel sits the Sister and the Mother and the Great-grandmother of Evil, the Holy One help us all, and we all of us know *that*, too! If she so chooses we'll have storms and leaks; and if she don't so choose we'll have an easy journey of it. That's no tale for tadlings, now—

40

that's same as saying the sun's more use to solar collectors than snow is."

There were two Michael Callaway Brightwaters standing near, one of them a 40th and the other a 37th, something of a nuisance in such close quarters. They hadn't much use for one another, or for Gabriel John, but they shook their heads like one man now and allowed as how he was absolutely right and the captain could leave off *his* tales any time.

"We're not fools," said the one they called Black Michael—not that his hair was any blacker than Michael Callaway the 37th's, that was called simply Michael Callaway in the ordinary fashion, but you couldn't be having them both speak up every time one was wanted. And Michael Callaway nodded, saying: "We came for the money, same as you, Captain. And what trouble we've got on our plates is trouble we bought ourselves. Complaining about it, that's not seemly; I agree to that. Howsomever, Captain, you'll do us the favor of telling us no lies, thank you very much."

The captain stared at the three of them, considering, and at the eloquent back of Haven McDaniels Brightwater the 4th, pretending to be fooling with a sail—him that had started all this—and he shrugged his shoulders.

"All right," he conceded. "I'll not dispute youall on it. I don't care for her myself . . . they say she was a child once, but I'm hard put to it to believe it. But I'll not listen to *prattle* over the matter, either, mind you. As Michael Callaway rightly says, this is our own doing, of our own free will, and talk'll change nothing. Furthermore and to go *on* with, such talk heard at the wrong end of the boat might well provoke the lady. You'll do *me* the favor of not chancing that. That's my last word!"

Truth was, he thought as he turned away from them with a set jaw intended to impress them with his firmness of purpose, the sight of her made his blood run colder than the seawater. No woman should stand six feet tall like she did; no woman should fit to a fishing-boat like she'd been born on one, when she'd spent her whole life in Castle and in mountain cabin; no woman should have the dark fierce beauty that somehow flamed around her, putting him in mind of the black roses that grew near the edge of Marktwain's desert in deep summer.

Anybody'd described her to him, and him not knowing, he'd of thought she'd stir his loins. Especially out on this b'damned ocean with no other woman for many a mile and many a long lonely night. Yet when he looked at Troublesome of Brightwater, for all the sweet curve of her breasts and hips and the perfection of her face, he would of sworn he could feel his manhood shriveling in his trousers. He'd as soon of bedded a tall stake of Tinaseeh ironwood.

That didn't mean he'd tolerate a dauncy and fractious crew, whatever the feelings she raised in him or in them. He'd keep the men too busy to have time left over for mumblings and carry-ons. He wanted to get this fool trip over with—he needed the money the Grannys had come up with, and how they'd done it he couldn't imagine, but it was none the less a fool trip for all that—and he wanted to find himself back in his own bed, cosy with his own wife, that was a soft round woman more his style. With a voice like the call of an Ozark house-dove just as the sun was coming up, and no more like that female in the stern than if they'd been different species altogether.

"You turn to," he barked over his shoulder at the men, "and I'll do my share, and we'll get this out of the way and be home to brag on it before we have time to think."

Nobody said "*if* we get home"; they weren't whiners. They'd been offered a fair sum of money badly needed, and they'd do the job it was offered for. Still, it was a sorry time of year to take to sea in a boat this size and age, Troublesome or no Troublesome. Had the boat been newer, that would of been a help; had it been larger, they couldn't have handled her with only the five, and that would *not* have been a good thing. It would cause a certain amount of fuss and feathers to drown five good men, for sure—but if they drowned a daughter of Castle Brightwater they'd set every Granny on Ozark whirling like a gig . . . that happen, they'd better hope they all drowned with her. It'd be more comfortable in the long run.

Behind the men, Troublesome chuckled under her breath, and Gabriel John jumped like he'd been pinched.

"Knows what we're thinking, that one does," he said flatly.

"And so does the Mule, and that doesn't bother you."

"*She* bothers me," insisted the man doggedly, "considering what I was thinking just then when she laughed."

The captain turned back and grabbed Gabriel John's shoulder in his fist. "That's one word too many," he said through his teeth. "*One word* too many! You guard your thoughts and keep 'em proper; and you sail this boat and keep your mind on your business. I don't intend to have to say any of this again."

As they'd said, there were certain stands he was obliged to take.

It happened that Troublesome did know what they were thinking. But not because of any telepathic powers, such as the Mules had, or the Magicians of Rank. No special powers were required to read those stiff backs with the muscles knotted round the necks—whopping headaches they were going to have, later on! —or the rigid shoulders, or their muttering back of their hands and out of the corners of their mouths. It amused her mightily to think that they could believe she had special skills and still be fretting about their hides; it showed a lack of common sense. After all, if this boat went down, she'd go down with it. Or perhaps it was their souls that they were really worried about, and not their hides; perhaps they thought the wickedness might blow off of her in the seawind and stick to them forever and ever more. She chuckled again, and watched the muscles in their backs twitch to the sound, before she turned her head to look out over the water.

She wasn't sure of what she'd seen out there, not yet.

Might could be it'd been only a trick of the light slanted on the water, such as had ages back made men think dragons swam in the oceans of Old Earth. Might could be it had been the squint of her eye against that light, or her irritation of mind. There was not a single reason to believe that a creature never seen since First Landing—seen then by a group of exhausted people that might have been over given to imagining—should choose to show up a thousand years later and swim alongside her to Kintucky. It was as unlikely a happenstance as had come her way within memory, and she wasn't going to assume it for gospel too quickly.

First, she'd wait for another sight of that great tail split three ways. And then probably she'd wait for the royal purple of the thing's flesh to show up clear in the gray of the sea. And when both had happened, assuming they did happen, she'd think it over—and might could be she'd go below and swallow a dose to cure her of her mindfollies.

The Teaching Story had not one word extra to spare on the subject of the creature she half thought she'd seen. The fuel on The Ship had gone bad. Every last thing had been going from bad to worse. The time had come when it was land or die; and then just as they made a desperate plunge toward the planet below them the engines gave up completely and The Ship fell into the Outward Deeps. At which point, as the Grannys taught it:

Even as the water closed over the dying ship and First Granny told the children to stop their cater-wauling and prepare to meet their Maker with their mouths shut and their eyes open, a wonderful thing happened. Just a *won*derful thing!

Forty of them there were, shaped like the great whales of Earth, but that their tails split three ways instead of two. And their color was the royal purple, the purple of majestic sovereignty.

They met The Ship as it fell, rising up in a circle as it sank toward the bottom. And they bore it up on their backs as easy as a man packs a baby, and laid it out in the shallows, where the Captain and the crew could get The Ship's door open, and everybody could wade right out of there to safety.

They were the Wise Ones, so named by First Granny; and it may be that they live there still in the Outward Deeps. . . .

And it may be that they don't. A thousand years ago, that was, that First Granny had looked into the huge eye of one of them and seen there something she claimed at once for wisdom, and no least sign of them since in all this long time. They could certainly all have died—long, long ago. If ever they were real, that is, and not an illusion born of desperation and nourished on Grannytalk.

No other Teaching Story made mention of them, and no song; not even a scrap of a saying referred to them. It made them *most* unlikely traveling companions! Why, even the creatures of Old Earth, those left-behind ones that nobody'd seen since before the Ozarkers left their home planet, came up now and again in sayings. Take the groundhog; what a groundhog might be, Trouble-

some couldn't have said. There was nothing whatsoever
in the computer databanks about them, nor anywhere
else. But she knew easy enough from the roles ground-
hogs took in daily converse that they couldn't of been
any kind of *hog*. "Quick as a groundhog down a hole!"
the Grannys would say. "No bigger'n the ear on a
groundhog!" "Saw its shadow and popped under like a
groundhog!" Had to of been little, and quick, and somehow significant; you could figure that out from the
scraps. But the creatures of the Outward Deeps? They
were mentioned nowhere at all, and what mysterious
purpose might bring one to be her escort now . . . She
sighed. It wasn't reasonable; but then her ignorance was
great.

Troublesome turned her head to the wind and took a
deep breath of the salt air to drown out some of the fish
stink, and gathered her shawls closer round her, wrin-
kling her nose as the blown spray spattered her face. It
would come up a rain shortly, she was sure, and the men
would be blaming her for it. Law, what wouldn't she
give to have had the weather skills they were willing to
lay to her account! Now *that* would of been of some
use. Dry fields she could of watered, and high winds taking off the good topsoil she could of tempered, and
where the rivers were bringing sullen rot to the roots of
growing things she could of driven back the clouds and
let the sun see to drying them out. There'd of been a
good deal less hunger on Ozark if she'd been able to
turn her hand to such work as that.

Instead of which, she thought, reality falling back
over her with a thump, she was off on the wildest of

goose chases, set her by seven dithering Grannys. Off to
see the Lewis Motley Wommack the 33rd.

No special wonder her sister had lusted after the man
and taken him so willingly to her bed. There was no
prettiness to him, no softness anywhere, but he was a
man to feast the hungry eyes on, not to mention a few
other senses. He gave off a kind of drawing warmth that
naturally made you want to shelter in it, male or female
—as she herself gave off a cold wind that said, *Stand
Back!* If lust had been one of the emotions known to
her she might very well have fancied him her own self;
in a kind of abstract fashion, she could see that. But
handy though he might be in a bed, the idea that some
act of his lay behind Responsible's sorry condition, or
that he could do anything to improve it . . . ah, that
was only foolishness. Troublesome had no hope for the
journey's end; she traveled to Kintucky for the excellent
reason that she'd never been there and might never have
a second chance, and because curiosity *was* one of the
emotions she was familiar with.

There were times, in point of fact, when she found
herself so curious about the workings of this world that
the lack of any source to ask questions of was almost a
physical pain. At such times, there being no purpose to
such a feeling, she was grateful for the mountain to take
out her energies on, and she welcomed the work given
her to do though she understood it scarcely at all. She
would go at her loom then with a vengeance, making
the shuttle fly, singing ballads so old she didn't know
what half the words meant. Unlike her sister, she could
sing to pleasure even the demanding ear, and when her

audience was only birds and small creatures she didn't mind doing it. There was nobody on the mountain to wonder at a female singing out "I go to Troublesome to mourn and weep" when the word was her very name, nor to pity her for the next line all about sleeping unsatisfied, nor to wonder as she changed tunes where Waltzing Hayme might be. She loved the queer ancient songs and valued them far above such frippery as was sung these modern days.

Thinking of it, she very nearly began to sing, and then remembered the five men—it would not do to have them hear her singing and carry the tale of it back to Brightwater. She closed her lips firmly on the riddling song she'd almost let escape, and resolved to close her mind just as tight to the questions running round there. She'd get no answers to them in her lifetime, and might could be it wasn't meant that humans should have those answers. Might could be, for instance, that they were the proper knowledge of the Wise Ones, kept in trust against a time when they might be needed. . . .

Granny Hazelbide, commenting to the little girls on the Teaching Story about the saving of the Ozarkers at First Landing, always said the same thing: "First Granny looked right into the eyes of one of them, just *right into its* eyes! And she said then and there, no hesitating and no pondering on it, 'They are the Wise Ones,' and no doubt that is so."

*Perhaps*, thought Troublesome. Perhaps. She'd seen eyes to creatures that looked to contain all the secrets of the universe. The feydeer, for example, along the ridges above timberline. They had eyes you could gaze into forever, and they had minds as empty as a shell left behind by its tenant and scoured out by a determined housewife. Rain gave them a fever that became a pneumonia and kept them few in number, but they hadn't sense enough to go down a few feet on the mountain where they could have stood beneath a tree or under a ledge out of the weather. They just waited, shaking and bedraggled, for the rain to kill them off. It gave the lie to those eyes, for all they looked so knowing.

She had a firm intention, if there was indeed a Wise One keeping this dilapidation of a boat company for some purpose of its own; and it was that intention that kept her here with her eyes fixed to the water, hour after hour. She wanted to look, her *own* self, "right into" the eye of the sea creature. It would be an eye to remember, if it were no more a gate to wisdom than the feydeer's! Judging by the tail she thought she'd caught a glimpse of, be the animal truly wise or truly foolish it was as big as this boat. The eyes would be . . . how big? The size of her head, with a pupil to match? Might could be. Law, to see that, to give it a look as it rose to dive, and to get a look back! That would be a thing to remember all her days and all her nights, and she had no intention of missing it if it came her way. She had no other chores; she would sit here and watch over the water for that exchange of glances, all the way to Kintucky and all the way back if need be.

The men turned surly eventually, as was to be expected. And after they'd seen Troublesome well onto the land the captain thought it prudent to let them talk it out of their systems while the boat rode at anchor.

They went on awhile about their various disgruntlements, allowing as how they were sorry they ever let the Grannys tempt them to this forsaken place. Allowing as how they'd never before seen a Mule swim the sea with a woman on its back and they called that witchery and they'd like to hear the captain deny them *that*. And they did a ditty on the short rations—as if they were any shorter than they'd been ashore—and another on the constant drizzling rain that had pursued them all the way and looked likely to pursue them all the way back, and they'd like to hear the captain deny them *that!*

Adam Sheridan Brightwater was wise in the ways of surly men; he denied nothing, made uninterpretable noises when they drew breath and seemed to expect a response, and let them wear themselves out. Only when they were reduced to muttering that if she hadn't been a woman, by the Holy One, they'd of gone off and left her and her bedamned Mule to fend for themselves did he add anything to the conversation. Seeing as there was no knowing how long they'd be there waiting for her, he thought it might be better to turn their minds from the idea of abandoning her in the Kintucky forests and heading for home.

"What do you suppose she was *looking* at back there all that time?" he threw out, rubbing at his beard. "That has got to be the lookingest woman ever I did see . . . and nothing to look at but water, water, and still more water. Thought her eyes would drop right out of her head."

"I don't know what it was she was staring after," Gabriel John answered him promptly, "but I know one thing—it never turned up, and she's given up on it."

"*How* do you know that?

"Heard her. This is a mighty small boat, if you hadn't noticed that already, for keeping secrets on."

"What'd she say?" demanded Black Michael, and when Gabriel John told them they whistled long and low.

"No woman says that," declared Haven McDaniels Brightwater.

"She *did*." Gabriel John was staunch as staunch. "Right in a string, she said it, three broad words such as I never heard before at one time in the mouth of a *man*. *And* I saw her give the gunwales a kick that I doubt did her foot much good. In a right smart temper, she was!"

"We could ask her," Michael Callaway proposed.

"Ask her? You enjoy being dogbit, Michael Callaway?"

"There's no dogs on this boat, you damned fool! Mules, but no dogs. Talk sense, why don't you!"

Black Michael gave him an equally black look and smacked his thigh with the flat of his hand and called *him* a damned fool.

"You ask her a question," he said, "she'll take your head right off at the armpits! Dogbit's not a patch on it, *I* can tell you. Why, I had the uppity gall to ask her highandmightyness could I help her with a jammed *hatch*, Michael Callaway, and I near lost part of my most valuable anatomy when she flung it back at me . . . you'd of thought I'd offered to toss her skirts up and tumble her, tall scrawny gawk that she is, and I meant her only a kindness! Huh! I say leave her alone, as the Grannys directed, and be grateful if she follows suit. Womanbit, that's what you'll be otherwise . . . or womankicked, or womanstung, or worse!"

Captain Brightwater nodded his agreement with that as a general policy, it being somewhat more than obvious, and the nods went slowly all round.

"Maybe she'll sight whatever it was on the way back after all," he said easily. "And maybe that'll make her pleasanter to be around. We can hope."

Troublesome, doing her best to keep the branches from whipping Dross into a refusal to go on through the Kintucky Wilderness, was not expecting any such thing. The tail she'd seen again, a time or two, and a flash of purple. Sufficient to prove that the animal was there and as real as she was. But had it meant her to see anything more, had it intended a shared glance, it would have happened by now, and she'd resigned herself to that. She'd not be staring over the water on the trip back, yearning after what she was not to have.

She only hoped they'd *make* it back to Marktwain. Glad as she was that they hadn't seen their huge companion, those stalwart sailing men, and determined as she was to let slip no careless word now or later, she was astonished. It seemed to her that they might well have trouble even finding Marktwain again, it being no bigger than a continent. What kind of sailors were they, that an animal the size of their boat could swim alongside them from one side of the ocean to the other, and them never even notice it? Come time to land again, she might have to point them out the coast or they'd sail right on past.

"*Disgusting*," she said to Dross, who said nothing back, but whuffled at her in a way Troublesome was willing to take for confirmation. "Plain disgusting!"

# CHAPTER 4

"I say we should use the lasers, and the devil take the treaties." The King of Farson Kingdom took a look at their faces and shivered in the cold, and he said it over again, louder and clearer, to be sure they'd heard him.

There'd been a day when a statement like that, all naked and unadorned and enough to shock the whiskers off a grown man's face, would have been cushioned somewhat by the rugs and draperies and furnishings of Castle Farson. No longer. The Castle had been stripped of everything that had any value, and it was nothing now but a great hulk of stone in which every word echoed and bounced from wall to wall and down the bare corridors. Any citizen choosing to look in the windows at the royal Family might do so; no curtains hung there. And the chair where Granny Dover sat pursing her lips at the King's scandalous talk was the only chair they had left; a rocker for the Granny in residence, and a courtesy to her old bones. As for the rest of them, they sat on the floor and leaned against the wall, or dragged up the rough workbenches that had once been out in the stables and now served for eating meals. When there *were* meals, which was far from always.

"Jordan Sanderleigh Farson the 23rd," said the Granny grimly—she'd never said "Your Majesty" to him nor ever would—"you've been hinting at that, and tippytoeing around that, these last three days now . . . but I never thought I'd live to hear you come right out and say it in so many words."

"And only blind luck that you *have* lived that long," the man retorted.

"No," said the old lady. "Many a thing as has changed in these terrible times, *many* a thing. Kings at Farson and Guthrie, 'stead of Masters of the Castle, as has been since First Landing and is decent and respectable! Three old fools at Castle Purdy calling themselves *Senators*, if you please, and splitting the Kingdom's governance three ways, when they never could run it even when it wasn't split and they had tradition to give 'em a clue what to do every now and again!"

"Granny, don't start," begged the King, but she paid him no mind whatsoever.

"But the day's not come yet," she went on, "when an Ozarker—always excepting the filthy Magicians of Rank, that, praise be, have had their teeth pulled anyway—when an Ozarker would raise a hand to harm a Granny. I'll be here a while yet, if we do live on weeds and bad fish. I'll be here a while."

Marycharlotte of Wommack, huddled against the draft in a corner more or less sheltered from the wind, challenged her husband and drew her shawl tighter round her shoulders.

"We gave our word," she flung at him, "as did Castles Guthrie and Purdy! We aren't degraded enough, living worse than animals in a cave—at least they have fur enough to keep them warm, or sense enough to sleep the winter out—we aren't degraded *enough*? Eating thin soup three times a day, made like the Granny says out of weeds and roots and one bad fish to a kettleful, and the Twelve Gates only knows what people not at the Castle must be living on! That's not enough for you yet? All the animals slaughtered, all the children and the old people sick, and the young ones fast joining them, that won't satisfy you men? Must we be liars and traitors as well, *before you've had enough?*"

Jordan Sanderleigh Farson turned his back on his Queen and spoke to the wall before him, down which a skinny trickle of water ran day and night from the damp and the fog.

"We cannot go on like this," he said dully.

"There's a choice?"

"We cannot go on fighting a war," answered the King, "grown men from a time when ships can travel from star to star and computers can send messages over countless thousands of miles . . . fighting a war with sticks, and boulders, and knives, and a handful of rifles meant for hunting or taken out of display cases at the museums. You should *see* it out there, you two . . . you're so smug, you should go take a long look. It's a giant foolery, entirely suitable for the comedy at a low-quality fair in a Purdy back county. Except that people are not laughing, you know. People are dying."

"I thought that's what you wanted," said Marycharlotte. "People dying."

"You made it right plain that was what you wanted,

all you men," Granny Dover backed her up. "No question."

The man leaned against the wall, whether it was despair or exhaustion or both they did not know, and shouted at the two of them.

"We never had any intention that it was to drag on and on and *on* like this!" he roared. "A week or two, we thought, maybe a month or two at worst and a few hundred dead, and then it would be *over!* This isn't what we meant to have happen . . . oh, the Holy One help me in a bitter hour, it was never what was intended, never!"

The two women, the one near a hundred years old and the other in the full bloom of her years, but both little more than bones wrapped in frayed rags, they kept their silence. He looked to them for the smooth moves to comfort that he expected, the reassurance that of course it wasn't his fault and he had done all he could and more than most would of been able to; and none of that was forthcoming. They didn't *say* to stop his whining . . . but he heard it nonetheless. Jordan Sanderleigh, raised on the constant soothing words and hands of Ozark women, felt utterly abandoned. This was indeed a new day, and a new time altogether, when the women of his own household looked at him like they would a benastied three-year-old.

"Jordan Sanderleigh," said the Granny, and she measured her words out one by one and hammered them in with the tip of her cane, "when this war began, a Solemn Council was held. All the Families of Arkansaw, there assembled. And it was agreed that we were

58

Ozarkers, not barbarians such as we left on Old Earth because we despised them worse than vermin! And it was agreed that in the name of decency, *to* which we still lay claim, I hope, no Arkansawyer would use a laser against another or against another's holdings. Signed it was, and sealed. And we'll not be the ones as goes back on it."

The man flung himself down on the nearest window ledge and closed his eyes. He remembered the occasion well. Himself, King of Farson; James John the 17th, King of Guthrie; the three Purdy Senators . . . the Granny was right that they were fools, all they could do was squabble among themselves, but they'd had dignity that day, the Purdy crest on their shoulders and their staffs of office in their hands. And the women, all absent to show their disapproval, but willing when it was over to admit that if there had to be a war it was a considerable improvement over the ancient kind for them to meet before it and set up its conditions. He had not been ashamed that day, and he had not been poor; he had been eager to get at the war, to settle once and for all the question of who should be first on Arkansaw, to be done with it and take up their lives once again. And he had been more than willing to sign that treaty banning the lasers . . . it was civilized.

"We all die, then," he said aloud. "Slowly. Like fools and lunatics."

The Granny hesitated not one second.

"So be it," she said.

"Ah, you women are hard," mourned the man.

59

"Ah, you men are fools. And lunatics." Marycharlotte of Wommack mocked him, matching her tones exactly to his. And he said nothing more.

Out in the ravaged Wilderness Lands of Arkansaw the struggle went on, as it had for near twelve months now. First there had been the preliminary squabbling, as each of the Castles moved to lay out that *it* should rule over all on Arkansaw henceforth, and be first among the three Kingdoms, and had thought to do that with words and threats and strutting about. There'd been no idiot behavior such as had disgraced Castle Smith, no purple velvet and ermine and jeweled scepters and Dukes and Duchesses—a King and a Queen, dressed as they'd always dressed, that had sufficed. But it had never occurred to either Farson or Guthrie that the two other Castles would argue about their obvious and predestined supremacy on the continent.

And then when it became obvious to everybody that neither Farson nor Guthrie would ever accept the other, and that Castle Purdy would never do more than wait to see which was the winner so that it could join that side, there had been the period of drawing back to the Castles to decide what was to be done. There had been the shameful ravaging of the tiny continent of Mizzurah off Arkansaw's western coast, both the Kingdoms of Lewis and of Motley, so that that land which had been the greenest and fairest of all Ozark now looked like the aftertime of a series of plagues and visitations of the wrath of some demented god. Not that Mizzurah had wanted any part in the feuds of Arkansaw, but that Arkansaw

60

had been desperate for even Mizzurah's pitiful resources.

And then the war had broken out—with the dignified meeting first, of course, to lay down the rules—and it dragged on still. Civil war.

When the citizens of Mizzurah had been ordered to join in the fighting on Arkansaw, they had made it more than clear that no amount of harassment would bring them to any such pass, so that it had been necessary for the Arkansawyers to take the Masters of Castles Motley and Lewis and hold them hostage at Castle Guthrie as surety against their people's obedience.

And now the men of Mizzurah fought alongside the men of Arkansaw, divided up three ways among the three Castles as was fair and proper, since it was that or see the hostages hung, or worse; but they spoke not one word, and they never would. In silence, they drew their knives, that had been intended for the merciful killing of herdbeasts, and used them on other Ozarkers as they were commanded, excepting always the delicate care they used to be sure they raised no hand against another Mizzuran. In the same silence they dropped great boulders from Arkansaw's cliffs down on columns of climbing men, and threw staffs of Tinaseeh ironwood to pin men against those cliffs for a death not one of them would have inflicted on *any* animal. The officers had the few rifles, and no Mizzuran was an officer, which meant they had no shooting to do, and that was probably just as well. The Lewises were without question the best shots on Ozark, having always fancied the sport of shooting at targets, and keeping it up over the centuries

61

when most of the Families had let the skill fall away into disuse.

The Mizzurah women fought beside their men, those not required back at home to care for tadlings and babes. "If the men must go, we go also," they'd said, and the women of Arkansaw, that would have nothing to do with the civil war among their men themselves, had nodded their heads in approval. It was fitting, and they would have done the same, had the situations been the same. They had been much embarrassed when a Purdy female, a tad confused about what was after all a complicated ethical question, took up an ironwood staff and marched off to join her older brother in the Battle of Saints Beard Creek; and it was the women of Castle Farson, happening to be closest, that had gone out and got the fool creature and brought her back to a willow switch across her bare buttocks, for all she was sixteen years of age. If that was what it took to make things clear at Castle Purdy, that was what it took, and they had not scrupled to do it.

Thirty men, two of them Mizzurans, were dug in at a mine entrance near the border of Farson Kingdom under the command of Nicholas Andrew Guthrie the 41st, on this day. Three days they'd been there now, and though water was plentiful it was fouled—that'd be the work of the Purdys, upstream—and the food was gone since the night before.

Their leader stared sullenly into the drizzle, and sat in the slimy packed layers of wet leaves at the mine-mouth, and would not be persuaded to go inside where it was at least dry.

"The sentries have to stay out here," he pointed out.

"You're not a sentry."

"All the same."

"It's foolishness," objected another Guthrie, close kin enough to offer open criticism regardless of rank. "What'll you gain that way, except pneumonia?"

"Pneumonia," said Nicholas Andrew Guthrie. "And I'll welcome it. Rather die that way than most of the other possibilities . . . at least it's an honorable death."

"Not if you leave your men without a leader by catching it, you blamed pigheaded fool!"

Nicholas Andrew Guthrie didn't even turn his head.

"What you talk there is the talk of a war that's real," he said, and spat to show his disgust. "This is no real war, and I'm no real leader, and youall're no real soldiers. And you'd be no more leaderless without me than you are while I sit here and court the passing germs, so shut your mouth."

"That's inspiring talk," said his cousin. "Really makes us all feel like throwing ourselves into the heat of battle, let me tell *you*."

"You want inspiration," said Nicholas Andrew, "you go home and get some. You'll get none out here. Here, you've got nothing whatsoever to do but wait for a Farson, or might could be some pitiful Purdy, lost as usual, to show up, so you can stick him through the gut with whatever's handy, or him you. Might could be you'd even have the privilege of doing your gutsticking on a

Mizzurah woman, just for the variety of the thing. And everybody can cut one more notch on the timber nearest them to signify the occasion. That inspire you? It doesn't inspire me, not the least bit."

There was a long silence, broken only by the constant nameless noise the drizzle made. And then a man spoke from behind them. "How many do you reckon there are left of us?" He had a festering sore on his leg, that would get no better in this damp, and a bandage to his shoulder, and he leaned against the mine wall to keep from falling. "How many, sir?"

*My brave and stalwart company*, thought Nicholas Andrew wryly. *My company of walking dead. Flourish of trumpets, roll of drums, off left.* Aloud, he said he didn't know.

"What with the bad food, and the sickness there's neither magic nor medicine to treat, and what with the cold, and this bleeding twelvesquare excuse for a war . . . there might could be two thousand of us, all told."

"Two thousand, Nicholas Andrew Guthrie!" The man staggered and clutched at nothing, and somebody moved quickly to grab the shoulder that wasn't hurt.

"Come on, now," said the kinsman hastily, "you don't mean that, and it's a downright cruel thing to say."

"Well, I stand by it," snapped Nicholas Andrew. "And if only a Purdy or a Farson'd come by this place, might could be we'd be able to make that one thousand nine hundred and ninety-nine."

There was silence behind him again, and he hoped it would last this time; he had no heart for talking to

64

them. The figure he'd named was a blind guess, but it could not be much more than that. Taking it in round numbers, there'd been ninety thousand of them when this began; fifty thousand Guthries, twenty thousand Farsons, and twenty thousand Purdys. At least sixteen thousand Lewises and Motleys combined, he'd hazard. And what was left would hardly make one good-sized village . . . and nothing gained for it, nor nothing *ever* to be gained. Over those centuries when violence was just something in stories and songs around the fire, and an evil something at that, the Ozarkers had forgotten what their native stubbornness would mean if it were put to violent purposes.

It meant nobody would ever yield. It meant nobody would ever give up, ever say, "All *right*, let's stop before every last one of us is dead in this mess. All *right—you* can be the winner, if that's what it takes to stop this!"

It would never happen. When only two Arkansawyers of different Kingdoms still remained alive on this land, they would be fighting hand to hand—with two rocks, if that was all they had left to fight with, as seemed likely. And it would be a fight to the death. It seemed sometimes that somebody ought to of remembered, when it started, what a war would be like when there could be *no giving up ever* . . . but nobody had.

The Gentles had no doubt gone deep into the bowels of the earth; not one had been seen since since the first day of the fighting. And if they simply waited there long enough, they would have Arkansaw back for their own again, what was left of it, without a single Ozarker to trouble them.

"I think I hear something," whispered a boy at his side, crawling up close to whisper it in his ear. "Want I should go take a look?"

"You step outside this mine-mouth," said Nicholas Andrew flatly, and right out loud, "and provided you did indeed 'hear something' you'll be picked off before your beautiful blue eyes can blink twice."

"Oh . . . I thought I could get out there, quick-like, and scout around."

Nicholas Andrew was so weary of explaining what two and two added up to, and explaining it to babes barely out of their diapers . . . He drew a long breath, and tried to sound patient.

"Supposing you did hear something, son," he said, "and supposing it was a human being and one fighting against us. Either he'll stay where he is, which'll do us no harm, or he'll come out into the open where we can pick him off from here—which'll do us no harm. If he made a noise, you can be sure the idea was to get one of *us* to come out and be picked off. Otherwise, he'd of kept quiet. You follow all that?"

"Yes, sir," said the boy. "Yes, sir, I do. I expect I'm mighty ignorant."

"I expect you're mighty young," said Nicholas Andrew. "Now get back inside where it's safer."

Ignorance. He thought about ignorance. His own military training had been composed of a speech made to a couple dozen like him. They'd all been told that war wasn't much different from hunting, always excepting what the quarry was, and that they'd been picked for their natural qualities of leadership and their good

66

health, and that they were expected to use their common sense. That had been the sum total of it.

At Castle Guthrie the state of despair was not quite so complete as it was out in the Wilderness Lands or at the other two Castles. Castle Guthrie had been richest to begin with; it was richest still, though its poverty was astonishing. And it had the two hostages, two living symbols that some real action had once been taken— Salem Sheridan Lewis the 43rd, and Halbreth Nicholas Smith the 12th, him as was husband to Diamond of Motley and Master of Motley Castle. Whether he would have stayed on as Master there after the Confederation of Continents was dissolved, or gone back to Smith Kingdom to join his kin, there'd not been time for anybody to find out. Before the issue could be resolved, he'd found himself hostage here; and might could be there were times when he was thankful for the curious chance of it. It would not of been easy for him to choose between his own household—his wife and his children—and his kin. Especially when his kin were known to out-Purdy the Purdys for stupidity.

Around the one fire they had burning in the Castle, the Guthries sat in Council. James John Guthrie the 17th, another threadbare King; Myrrh of Guthrie, his sixth cousin and his queen as well; Michael Stepforth Guthrie the 11th, Magician of Rank (for all that signified these days) ; three older sons and an odd cousin or two.

They were not discussing the possibility of bringing into this war the cruel and efficient lasers, of which every

Arkansaw Family had a plentiful supply, used to shape Tinaseeh ironwood and work Arkansaw mines and quite capable of cutting a man into strips no thicker than a sheet of pliofilm. They were not yet reduced to considering such measures, unlike the Farsons, for they had one hole card left to them still. They were discussing the question of whether a Guthrie ship might be put to use.

"We only have men enough left to send one medium-sized ship, maybe a Class C freighter," Michael Stepforth was saying, "but one is all we ought to need, and a Class C quite big enough. We send it in to Brightwater Landing, we take the Castle, we get ourselves a computer and a comset transmitter and three or four technicians that know how to assemble and run those, grab whatever they tell us we have to have in the way of equipment—and back we come. Why not?"

"You think Brightwater'd let us get away with that?" demanded Myrrh of Guthrie. "It's a far sight from being what I'd call a *secret* operation."

"We don't have any reason to believe Brightwater even knows there *is* war on Arkansaw," said her husband. He gave the high stone hearth an irritated kick with the toe of his boot, and then did it again for good measure. "For all they know, we're fat and prosperous over here, living peacefully and respectably, sitting round the tables tossing off strawberry wine and reminiscing about the olden days."

"Goatflop," pronounced Granny Stillmeadow. Elegance had never been her strong suit. "I suppose they think snow doesn't fall here, nor diphtheria touch the babies, nor rivers ever go to flood, nor any *other* such ordinary human catastrophes. I suppose they think we Arkansawyers are immune to all such truck. Goatflop!"

"All right," said the King, "I'll grant you that's not reasonable. I'll grant you that wasn't the brightest speech I ever made."

"That's mighty becoming of you," snorted the Granny. "Seeing as how it was beyond question the *stupidest* speech you ever made, and not for lack of other examples to choose from."

"Granny Stillmeadow," said the man, "you can granny at me all you like, and no doubt I deserve it. But it still holds that they have no reason, none whatsoever, to be suspicious of one of our ships at their Landing. If they think we're starving over here, they'll be just that more likely to think we've come to beg for food, and I say *let* them—just so as we get inside the Castle."

They thought about that a while. It was true, there'd been no communication between the other continents and Arkansaw—it was barely possible that, with the comsets out and the Mules not flying, the war on Arkansaw was as much a secret to the Brightwaters as conditions on Kintucky were to the Families of Arkansaw. It was not something you could test, one way or the other. The war took up so much of *their* minds that there was a sneaking tendency to consider it the major preoccupation of everyone else on Ozark as well . . . but that was clearly foolish. Childish. Might could be everybody knew, and what they thought of it would not be anything to pleasure the ear. And might could be nobody knew except the sorry citizens of Mizzurah, that had suffered its effects directly. There was no way of knowing.

And it was true that nobody but Brightwater and Guthrie had had ships of a size adequate for ocean transport, and Guthrie still had its ships; putting one of them to use was something open to them, however much it might strain the last fragments of their supplies and energies.

"Think, Granny Stillmeadow," said Michael Stepforth Guthrie. "Think what it would mean, if it worked."

"With computers, and computer technicians to run them, we'd have just enough of an edge," put in one of the sons. "Just enough to turn things around, Granny."

Yes. They would be able to offer the remnants of the population of Arkansaw quite a few things, if they had the computers. And *do* to them quite a few things, if they seemed reluctant to accept the benefits offered.

"It's everything wagered on one throw," said Granny Stillmeadow, "I remind you of that. We might send a ship once; we might get into the Castle once . . . but there's only the once. And I remind you that even that piddling chance is a matter of pure ignorant luck, no more! We've not so much as a Housekeeping Spell to set behind it as a prop-up, don't you forget that!"

"So? Our luck is not as good as anybody else's?"

The Granny made a noise like a Mule whuffling, and brought her knitting needles to a full stop, and stared at him in a mixture of contempt and disbelief that had an eloquence words would be hard put to it to match.

"Coming from you, Michael Stepforth," put in Myrrh of Guthrie, "that *does* sound half-witted. I'll back the Granny on that. We may all have started even, so far as luck was concerned, when we began this—everything fair and square. But when we brought the Masters of Lewis and Motley into this Castle and put them under guard, them as had no quarrel with us nor ever wanted any, nor ever raised a hand against any Arkansawyer . . . then we changed that luck considerably."

"Purdy and Farson were in on that, too!"

"Purdy and Farson don't have the hostages—Castle Guthrie has them," said the Granny grimly. "A Guthrie stands guard by their doors. A Guthrie takes them their rations, and checks to be sure their bonds are adequate. Not a Purdy, my friends, not a Farson—that is our *personal* contribution, done on our own resolve, and volunteered for, as I recollect. Nobody forced it on us. And for *that*, you mark my words, we will pay."

"We *have* paid!" James John Guthrie looked more a madman than a monarch, roaring at the Granny and shaking his fists. But she was not impressed one whit.

"And we will pay more," she told him. "I wouldn't send a rowboat across a rain puddle myself, the way the Universe is stacked against this Family at this particular point in time. As for taking all the men we have left as are strong enough to fight, and all the supplies called for to last them to Brightwater, and sending them off in a ship across the Ocean of Remembrances? Pheeyeew! Why not go dig up a Gentle and shoot it, James John Guthrie? Why not jump off the Castle *roof*, for that

71

matter, and be done with it? It'd be quicker and cleaner."

The Granny shoved her rocker back and stood up, very slowly and carefully. Her arthritis was tormenting her, and she had a crick in her neck that was about to drive her wild, from staring up at the Guthrie men while she tongue-lashed them.

"You think it over good and long before you decide," she said, trying not to let the pain overrule the contempt in her voice as she struggled to straighten her spine. "You think it over good and long and thorough. Might could be you ought to pray over it, too—I know *I* would. Take yourselves down to where Salem Sheridan Lewis the 43rd, that good man, that *honorable* man, sits a prisoner in your Castle, and ask him to pray with you. . . . I reckon you've forgotten how, these many days past. And when your minds are made up, do me a favor—keep it to your own selves. If you decide on any such folly as that expedition off to Never-never Land, don't you tell me about it; I don't care to know."

"Granny Stillmeadow," sighed the King of Guthrie, "you're no help at all, you know that?"

"I should hope I am not any help to you, I never intended to be for one *in*stant! Myrrh of Guthrie, you plan to sit there and listen to these idiot males go on with their claptrap, or you want to come with me and see if there's maybe some small thing we can do upstairs for that tadling down with the fever?"

Myrrh of Guthrie looked around her once, and then she didn't hesitate.

"I'll be right with you, Granny," she said.

"I'll go on ahead," said Granny Stillmeadow. "The air's cleaner outside this room."

And with that she turned around and stalked out, leaning on her cane and striking the floor with it every step like a stick coming down hard on a drumhead. There was no possibility of mistaking the Granny's opinion of them. Even with nothing to go on but the sight of her aching back.

# CHAPTER 5

Lewis Motley Wommack the 33rd was feeling reasonably content with his lot. He would have gone to some pains not to admit it, since the rest of the population was of a much different mind, but he found the current spartan regime exactly to his taste. The rooms of Castle Wommack—all four hundred of them—had always given him a vague feeling of claustrophobia; he knew why now. It had been all that furniture. The massive benches lining every hall, and the huge tapestries behind them. The draperies that you could have easily made a tent for five or six people out of, with the green velvet with twelve inches of gold fringe . . . and the occasional variety of *gold* velvet, with twelve inches of green fringe. The vases of flowers and the paintings in their heavy frames, and the thick carpets, all four hundred of *them* . . . no, he took that back. There had never been carpets in the kitchens. Make it three hundred and ninety-seven carpets. He had been smothered by all that, but he hadn't realized it; after all, in rooms thirty feet square, with fourteen-foot ceilings, the furnishings had been scattered around in a lot of empty space—as he recalled, there'd been a deliberate effort expressed by his cousin Gilead to keep the Castle's decoration "spare."

That had been her word, and he'd assumed it had some congruence with reality.

But now that it was all gone he realized that he could at last breathe freely. He liked the feel of the bare stone floors under his feet, and the look of the arched high windows open to the air and sky. He no longer felt that he had to go out and pace the balconies in the middle of the night, he was contented to pace his own almost empty room instead.

As for his once elegant wardrobe, now only a memory, and the diet of grains and root vegetables and ingeniously concocted soups that had replaced the roasts and stuffings and steaks and lavish desserts . . . he had never cared about such things anyway.

And at the moment he had several specific things to be happy about. There was, for instance, the blissful ease of his mind. At first he had been like the man with a toothache that comes and goes, always braced for the next twinge out of nowhere. Now, enough time had gone by since the last intrusion from Responsible of Brightwater that he felt *secure* in his privacy. She had been a parasite coiled in his head, never mind how many hundreds of miles of physical space separated them, and he had lived in constant dread of the stirring of that . . . thing . . . within him; it was gone, praise the Twelve Gates and the Twelve Corners, forever.

And there was the fact that Thomas Lincoln Wommack the 9th was now Master of this Castle, and had lifted from Lewis Motley's unwilling neck the burden of Guardianship that had chafed it so mightily since the death of Thomas Lincoln's father. He had detested being Guardian, and everything that went with it—all that constant fiddling detail—and he was firmly determined that never again would he have to administer so much as a dollhouse, or be responsible for anything more than his own person. His sister Jewel had the Teaching Order that had replaced the old comset educational system well in hand, and showed a natural talent for administration that he recognized as invaluable. He didn't even have to worry about *that*.

Bliss, basically. Impoverished bliss, perhaps, and a nagging concern for the problems of sickness and crop failures and the like that plagued Kintucky—but it had to be admitted that all of that was out of his hands and beyond his power to alter in any way. What he could do, he did; mostly, it amounted to encouraging Jewel of Wommack and her flock of Teachers in *their* efforts, all far more productive than his could have been. The ways they found to stretch supplies, and the things they thought of when there was pain to be eased . . . He admired it, loudly and openly and enthusiastically. And he thanked the Powers that none of it required anything more of him personally than that unflagging enthusiasm. Enthusiasm, he could always produce.

Thinking about it, a bowl of hot oats and half a cup of milk comforting his stomach, he leaned back in his chair and put his feet up on his desk, folded his arms behind his head, and sighed a long sigh of satisfaction.

At which point, his door flew open without so much as a warning knock, and he found himself facing a woman taller than he was, thinner than he was, and looking much the worse for wear, though it was clear she was beautiful underneath the scrapes and the grime. It took him only a couple of minutes to recognize Troublesome of Brightwater—there was only one woman on the planet who looked like she looked—and that was such a shock that he leaped to his feet and knocked his chair over in the process.

"Uhhhh . . . Troublesome of Brightwater!" he managed, and bent to pick up the chair and set it right.

"As you live and breathe," she said.

"Well, I know it wasn't exactly a fanfare and a red carpet, Troublesome, but you took me by surprise. I thought you spent all your time on top of a mountain and never came down except for emergencies . . . like clearing a pack of rats and weasels out of Confederation Hall, for example. Not to mention that however in the world you got *here*, all the way from Brightwater, is beyond me. Surely you didn't expect me not to be surprised?"

"May I come in or not?" Troublesome demanded. "Finding you wasn't easy, young man, and I'm sick of prowling your halls in search of your august presence."

"Please do come in," said Lewis Motley readily enough. "I'm . . . well, no, I can't say I'm delighted to see you. We'll no doubt end by regretting that you dropped by, I'm aware of that. But I am most assuredly *interested* to see you. . . . Do come in, and sit down."

Troublesome's eyes flicked over the room, and she clucked her tongue in amazement.

"What is it?"

"All this furniture." She stepped inside and closed the door behind her. "Brightwater's got a rocker for the

Grannys, and beds all around, and that's about it. Everything else has gone for firewood long ago."

"I was just thinking how *bare* it was. And how much I liked it bare."

"A matter of your point of view, I expect," said Troublesome. "It looks mighty grand to this pair of eyes."

"You're on Kintucky," he reminded her. "How, I don't know—we'll come back to that. But on Kintucky we could burn fires day and night for a hundred years and we'd still only have cut down the undergrowth. If we could eat trees, we'd be well fed here."

Troublesome reached for the offered chair, turned it backwards so she could lean her arms and chin on its back, and stared at him until he began to feel uncomfortable. And then it dawned on him why he felt that way, and he hollered till he got a servingmaid's attention and told her to bring up some food and drink.

"Not that it'll be much," he warned her. "Bread, I expect. And coffee, if we're lucky and Gilead's set some by for the odd special occasion."

"Considering it's been near on two days since I've had anything but water . . . and you do have glorious water on Kintucky, I meant to comment on that . . . I'm not likely to complain. And the Mule I left in your stable was not the least bit ungrateful for what he was getting there."

"The Mule," mused Lewis Motley Wommack. "You came in by Mule, did you? Now, Troublesome, I don't mean to seem to doubt your word, but—"

"Just from the coast," she sighed. "One leg after another, solid on the ground. The rest of the trip was in a pathetic beerkeg that's got the nerve to call itself a ship, and for which the only good word I've got to offer is that it didn't sink on the way over here. No doubt it'll make up for that oversight on the trip back, always providing it'll still even *be* there when the Mule and I trek back down to the shore. No, Lewis Motley Wommack, I am not claiming I can get a Mule to fly; I had trouble enough getting it to move at all."

"Well, it might have been that you could. Considering your reputation."

Troublesome let that pass, and he went on.

"*Will* you tell me why you're here and how you got here?" he insisted; he was rapidly running out of patience. "It's about as likely as a goat playing a dulcimer, you know. I think I'm entitled to an explanation."

"Passel of Grannys sent me," said Troublesome. "They near killed themselves, poor old things, getting up Mount Troublesome to talk me into it and then back down again. And they used up everything they had left in this world to bribe the captain of that purely pathetic boat and his patheticker crew, and putting together supplies enough for this carry-on. The supplies they meant me to have while I rode the Mule here, those *I* left for bribe, along with a trinket or two, to keep my trusty friends from heading back to Brightwater and stranding me here. And the Holy One defend them if they do strand me . . . if I have to *swim* back, I'll find them, every last one of them, and they'll rue the day they ever did any such a misbegotten trashy thing."

"Oh, they'll be there," said Lewis Motley.

"You think so?"

"You put it very well," he said, looking at the ceiling. "I doubt very much they'd care to have your lifelong vengeance on their coattails, Troublesome of Brightwater."

"Let us hope you are right," said Troublesome grimly. "For their sakes, and everybody else's."

"How does everybody else figure into it?" he asked, and she passed along the Grannys' tale to him, while he sat there shaking his head. For a while it was his wonderment at the Grannys going to all this trouble and expense, and Troublesome going along with it, for no more motivation than some old tea leaves and a gold ring on a thread in a stray wind. And then when it began to be clear to him that it had to do with Responsible of Brightwater, it was his dis-ease at the position he was being put in. True, this was Responsible's infamous sister; and true, if there was anything bodacious to do, she'd either done it or invented it. But there was such a thing as tattling, and there were certain kinds of tattling that were even more despicable than other kinds, and he felt like a skinnywiggler on a hot rock before she got to the end of it.

"Hmmmmm," he said, by way of response, and fooled around with his beard some. And then "hmmmm" again.

Troublesome gave him a measuring glance, and cleared her throat. "If it's your gallantry as is causing you pain, Lewis Motley, you can set that aside. The Grannys already told me Responsible lost her maidenhead during the Jubilee, and seeing as how you were there at the time and footloose, and seeing as how you are the most spectacular example of manflesh I ever laid eyes on, I do believe I can add up two and two and come out with four. And if I already know you were bedding my sister, we can perhaps just acknowledge that and move on to something more significant."

Lewis Motley cleared *his* throat, and blessed the fates that had put this female on Brightwater and him clear across an ocean away from her.

"Well?" she asked him. "Does that simplify matters for you some?"

"It does," he began, and was much gratified that the servingmaid came in just then with the bread and the coffee and gave him a chance to collect himself.

"Yes," he said again, when he'd got his breath back. He took a drink of the coffee and made a face; it wasn't much more than troubled water, weak the way they made it to stretch the last of the beans, and grain added in with a liberal hand. "That was abrupt, but it did ease my mind. I wouldn't have felt justified in telling you that, but if you know it already we've cleared the air. Now what *exactly* is the question the Grannys think I know the answer to? Because I warn you, Troublesome of Brightwater—I doubt it."

Over her shoulder he saw the flash of a long robe in the hall, through the door the servingmaid had left decently open instead of shut tight as she'd been shocked to find it, and he called out for his sister to join them. He knew the look of that robe, though he wasn't aware it was exactly the color of his eyes, by a frayed place at the back of the hem that came from too many hours spent on Muleback. It would be useful to have his sister here as a buffer between himself and Troublesome, now the indelicate part of the conversation was past; furthermore, he enjoyed showing her off.

"Jewel!" he called to her. "We've got company—come see!"

"Company?" She stepped in the door, one hand on the sill, the long sweep of her sleeve falling almost to the floor. "Are you wasting my time with foolishness again, Lewis Motley?"

Troublesome gasped, and clapped both hands to her mouth, and through her fingers she said, "Jewel of Wommack, I declare I never in all this world would of known you!"

The grave eyes of a woman grown looked back at her, that had been a child's eyes so short a time ago, calm, and possessed of a natural authority. The copper hair was hidden away completely under the wimple, and most of the face as well, but Jewel was all the more beautiful for the mystery the Teacher's habit lent her. For the first time she could remember, Troublesome of Brightwater was uncomfortably aware that she herself could do with a change of clothes and a tidy-up.

"Troublesome of Brightwater," said the Teacher, the first of all the Teachers. "I never thought to see you again, and now here you are. . . . What brings you here?"

"She's just about to set me a question," said her brother. "Sent here by the Grannys of Marktwain assembled, on a mountaintop no less, for that precise purpose. You sit down with us, sister mine, and have a cup of this terrible coffee, and if I can't answer the question perhaps you can help me a tad.

"It has to do with Responsible of Brightwater," he added, as if it were an afterthought of an afterthought, and he watched Jewel's lashes drop to shield her eyes as she took the third chair and poured her coffee.

"The Grannys know full well," said Troublesome, seeing no reason to waste time, "that the magic they were able to do was done on mighty puny power. But they were sure enough they were right to put this expedition of one together, and sure enough to convince me to try it. Jewel of Wommack, they are of the opinion that your brother knows how it came about that Responsible of Brightwater has been in a sleep like unto death these past two years. And if he knows that, they believe, it just might could be he'll also know how she can be waked up."

She looked at the man, in a silence so thick she could have stirred it with her coffee spoon, and then at his sister, and her heart sank.

"Ah, Dozens!" she said despairingly. "Dozens! You didn't even *know*, did you? I can tell, just looking at you! Without the comsets, and Kintucky out here on the edge of nowhere, and no travelers anymore . . . I suppose nobody on Kintucky knows. Ah, the waste of all this! Bloody Bleeding *Dozens!*"

Lewis Motley was so taken aback he couldn't have spoken a word, or moved, but Jewel of Wommack reached over and took the other woman's hand in both of hers.

"Tell us," she said, in the voice that every Teacher

84

was trained to use, or sent to do research and keep out of the classrooms if she couldn't. It was a voice that could not be disobeyed because it left no possible space for disobedience.

"My sister," said Troublesome, and because the exhaustion in her face frightened both the Wommacks, Lewis Motley shouted again for a servingmaid and demanded the last of their whiskey, "just into summertime, after the Jubilee, fell into a kind of sleep. Or a coma. . . . To look at her, you would think she was dead, but she has no sickness, and the name Veritas Truebreed Motley puts to it is *pseudocoma*. Just a sleep that does not end and cannot, so far as we've been able to tell, be ended. And since the day it began, everything has gone from bad to worse on Marktwain and Oklahomah; we hear there is *war* on Arkansaw. What may be going on in the rest of the world nobody knows . . . or even if there is a rest of the world any longer. Since the trouble started with whatever happened to my sister, the Grannys are convinced that there's a connection there— that if we could wake Responsible there would be hope for Ozark again. And they were certain—certain sure!— that Lewis Motley Wommack had the key to it. . . . Law, but they're going to be in a state over this, and I don't blame them, I don't blame them one least bit!"

"Just a minute, Troublesome," said Jewel.

"If Lewis Motley Wommack didn't even know about this," insisted Troublesome, "then the Grannys have made a mistake to end all mistakes, and a minute—nor a dozen minutes—won't change that."

The servingmaid came running with the whiskey, and

Jewel poured it out with a level hand and passed Troublesome of Brightwater the glass.

"You drink that," she said calmly. "And then, let's us *ask* him. Before we decide to speak of mistakes and waste and the end of the world, let's just ask him. Might could be he knows more than you think he knows, provided the questions are put to him properly."

Lewis Motley had his whole face buried in his hands, and they could see the muscles of his arms straining under the cloth of his sleeves.

"Never mind throwing chairs, dear brother," warned Jewel emphatically, keeping a wary eye on him. "This is not the time nor the place."

"*Curse them!*"

The bellow shook the lamp hanging above their heads, and although neither Troublesome nor Jewel jumped, they both had to grip their chairs not to.

"Curse them all, the *idiots!* I never had any such thing in mind—they must all have been crazy! Oh, if I could only get my hands on them, if I could just—"

Troublesome looked at Jewel of Wommack. "He knows something," she said, over the din. "He knows something after all."

"He knows everything, from the sound of his conniption fit," said Jewel coldly. "Now it's just a matter of getting it out of him . . . once he's worn himself out. Talk of *women* having hysterics!"

"I've been a damned fool," said her brother.

"Not for the first time, nor yet the hundred and first."

"But this time is exceptional."

"Then the sooner it's admitted to, the sooner we'll

know if it can be mended. I suggest you tell us what you've gone and done, Lewis Motley."

"Can I have some of that whiskey?"

"You can *not*. That's for medicine, and precious little we have left of it! There's nothing wrong with you but temper, and if you haven't died of temper before this you won't die of it today. Just speak up."

Lewis Motley sighed a long sigh, and began. "Your sister," he said to Troublesome, "was causing me a good deal of . . . misery."

Troublesome was dumbfounded.

"Misery? In what way, causing you misery? She was clear back on Marktwain, you were all the way over here on Kintucky."

"I hesitate to say it of her—"

"Say it!" commanded Troublesome.

"Your sister would not grant me privacy of mind," he said then, and the words fell, quaint and formal, in the stillness of the room.

"Lewis Motley," said Jewel simply, "you are either mocking us or you are stalling for time, and whichever one it is, it's not to be borne."

"No, I am not!" he protested. "Responsible of Brightwater *mind*spoke me"—she had gone far beyond just mindspeech, but he would not talk of that before two women, even to defend his actions—"every day, day after day after day, till I was nearly mad with it. I would be sitting working, I would be eating, I'd be seeing to a problem in the stables, I'd be talking as I am now, with one of the Family . . . and suddenly she was there, in my mind." He shuddered. "There've been

87

many females that tried to tag along after me, but they had at least the decency to do it in the flesh, where a person could see them and have a fair chance at getting away. Not Responsible of Brightwater! Oh no—not that one."

"And so you did what?" Troublesome held her breath, waiting.

"I sent for the Magicians of Rank, and asked them all to come here on a matter concerning Miss Responsible of Brightwater, which they were willing enough to do, let me tell you; and I told them what she'd done— because she'd gone far, far *past* the bounds of decency —and I asked them to make her stop. *That's* what I did. But not for the smallest wrinkle of time did I intend anything of the sort you've described to me, Troublesome. I meant them to reason with her, threaten her perhaps, set a small Spell on her . . . just stop her unspeakable mucking about in *my mind!* Never did I mean them to hurt her. . . . Jewel, tell her. Little sister, explain to this woman that I never meant them to do her harm."

Jewel of Wommack nodded, her eyes the color of river ice in late afternoon.

"He is mischief incarnate," she said slowly, in grave agreement, "but he would not do anybody deliberate harm. He simply does not *think*—he never did. And now, because of his selfish temper, if the Grannys are right we have this dreadful time of trouble all to be laid at my brother's feet. For all time. Congratulations, to the Wommack Curse!"

Troublesome gnawed at the end of her thick black

braid, dust and leaves and all, a gesture Thorn of Guthrie had tried in vain to break her of.

"Lewis Motley Wommack," she said carefully, "what did Responsible say to you when you asked her to stop it? Did she just refuse, say no, flat out with no explanation? That's not like her . . . not that any of it is like her . . . but what did she *say* to you?"

The man's face went cold and hard, and now it was Jewel's turn to clap her hands to her mouth, because she suddenly understood, before the answer came.

"I never asked her," he told them, voice like granite and a face to match. "She was *in* my mind; she knew how it repulsed me. . . . It would have been a very cold day in a truly hot place before I stooped to beg that vile little—before I stooped to ask Responsible of Brightwater to stop her foul behavior. *Ask* her, indeed—what do you think I am?"

Troublesome stood up and went over to a window, turned her back on him and on the Teacher, and stood staring out into the tangled woods beyond. She was shaking from head to foot, and her teeth gritted to keep them from chattering, in spite of the whiskey, and not until she had it under control did she turn round again, even through the spectacular bout of tongue lashing that Jewel of Wommack turned on Lewis Motley with. He had been told in baroque detail what an utter, despicable, pathetic, unspeakable, pigheaded, stupid, fool *male* he was, with elaborations and codas and emendations to spare, before Troublesome said another word. And when she did speak, her voice was hoarse with rage restrained.

"Lewis Motley Wommack," she said, "I cannot explain this, and I shan't try. I have no way of knowing the truth of it; I never knew even that Responsible had the skill of mindspeech. But I swear to you, and I know whereof I speak: my sister would never have knowingly done what you say she did. If she did it, she was bewitched, or mad, or anything else you fancy—but she would not have *done* that. Saving only Granny Graylady, there's not an Ozarker alive more scrupulous about privacy than my sister. And you . . . you never even asked her. You couldn't *stoop*, to one small question. Lewis Motley, I would not be you and bear the burden of guilt that you will bear. Not for any power in this Universe."

"I tell you—" he began, but Jewel's hand came down hard on his arm and silenced him.

"You've told us," said Troublesome. "You've told us all I care to hear from you. You've answered the question I came to ask, and the Grannys were right. It took all the Magicians of Rank to put my sister to sleep, apparently; it will no doubt take all of them together now to wake her up. *All* of them; now when the ships are not running the oceans, and the Mules are not flying, and the Magicians of Rank are scattered to the four corners of the world . . . four of them somewhere in the wilds of Tinaseeh, if they still breathe. And somehow, we will have to get them all together at Brightwater and have them undo this awful thing. And I'd best get on with it. The crew was half mutinous all the way here. Not a cloud came up they didn't charge me with having caused it just by being on their leaky old rowboat—I'm

not anxious to leave them waiting for me any longer on
your coast."

"I'll ride with you," said Lewis Motley at once. "I
know the shortest ways—we'll save time."

Jewel of Wommack stood up, put one slender finger
in her brother's chest, and pushed. It was a measure of
his state of mind that it brought him to a full stop; or-
dinarily, he was about as easy to stop as an earthquake.

"You will not," she said flatly. "You've done enough.
You've done so much more than enough already, my beloved brother, that your name will go down in history—
be satisfied with that. You may well have destroyed an
entire world for the sake of your pride—be satisfied with
that. And I will ride with Troublesome of Brightwater
to the coast to see if her ship has waited for her. And if
it hasn't, I will see to it that a way is found to get her
home, if I must call in every man still able-bodied on
Kintucky to turn his hand to shipbuilding."

"I would feel better if—"

"No doubt you would!" she cut him off. "I haven't
any interest in you feeling better. You have a lifetime
ahead of you to spend trying to ease your guilt, but *I'll*
not help you! And besides that, they wouldn't obey you,
Lewis Motley. Not as they will me, if that proves need-
ful."

Lewis Motley closed his eyes and made no more ob-
jections. She was right. Not a man on Kintucky that
would not, if a Teacher asked it of him, build a ship or a
cathedral or a rocket or anything else she might demand. It had been planned that way, and it had gone
according to plan; the Teachers were not just respected,

they were reverenced. He could not command that sort of loyalty.

And then . . . there was the way his head was whirling. It could not be true, but what if it were? What if Responsible had not known, really had not known, what she was doing to him? And he had not even given her the chance to stop?

He had seen it himself, it was what had led him to her bed, scrawny plucked creature that she was; there had been something special about her, and he had been determined to investigate it. Was it his curiosity, and his pride, that had made Ozark a wasteland . . . and how many deaths lay at his door?

He could not have ridden to the coast, he realized, as the two women left the room and slammed its door behind them. He could not, at that moment, have risen from his chair.

# CHAPTER 6

It was cold at Castle Brightwater; bitter bone-stabbing cold, the cold that comes when the skies are full of snow that refuses to fall; and the sky was a leaden sorrowful gray. No fires burned in any of the Castle fireplaces. The people in the towns and on the farms were better off by far than those at the Castle, because it had been for the most part a clear and sunny winter, and the solar collectors on their roofs had been adequate to carry them even through days like this one. The problems of keeping warm a hulking stone Castle designed with all the traditional drafty corridors and stairways were considerably more formidable.

Troublesome had gone through the gloom of the Castle like a wind added to the drafts that already whined there, with a fine disregard for the staff scuttling out of her way and the just-barely tolerance of the Family, shouting for Veritas Truebreed Motley the 4th, the Castle's very own Magician of Rank. "Where *is* the man?" she had demanded as she tore up and down the halls and through the parlors, and "Where has he *gotten* to?" She got nothing for her troubles but shrugs and raised eyebrows, but she was accustomed to that; ten years' practice being shunned toughened you up some.

She found him at last, by the simple expedient of

looking everywhere there was, up on the Castle roof rubbing his hands together and cursing fluently in a spot where a tower kept off the wind but let the dim light by.

"It's a fine thing," he observed, glaring at her, "when it's warmer outside the place you live in than it is *inside*, in the dead of winter. I've a good mind to move into that hotel down by the landing—I'd be more comfortable there, and I'm sure the company would be better. How did you find me, anyway?"

"Used an algorithm," said Troublesome.

He made a face, not appreciating that word in her mouth, and went on as if she'd not used it. "And it's finer *yet*, when a man can't even find privacy on the bestaggering roof of a bestaggering *Castle!* First, it was one of the Grannys; and then it was Thorn of Guthrie—curse her narrow pointy little soul—and now, the Twelve Gates defend us all, it's *you!* What's next, ghosts and demons?"

"Morning, Veritas Truebreed," said Troublesome calmly. "Nice to see you, too, I'm sure."

"What do you want with me?" the Magician of Rank demanded, cross as a patch. "Whatever it is, the answer is either no, I can't or no, I won't—there aren't any other answers at the moment."

"Might could be you're right," she said, "and might could be you're wrong. Long as we're being all binary here."

"Troublesome, you'll provoke me," he warned her, and she let him know how alarmed she was at that prospect.

"Besides which," she added, "you were already pro-

94

voked before ever I set foot on this roof. And you may go right on being provoked till you choke, for all I care."

"Well?" Veritas Truebreed was blue with cold and purple with outrage, but he knew quite well she could outlast him. "Speak up, woman; what are you here tormenting me for?"

Troublesome looked him up and down, noting that he'd abandoned the elegant garments of his station for something that looked more like a stableman's winter wear. Something nubby and bulky, with a thick lining and a narrow stripe and a capacious hood. It showed good sense on his part.

"I want you to wake up Responsible," she told him.

"You want me to what?"

"I've been to Kintucky and back, Veritas, and I—"

"You've been to *where?*"

"*As I said*, Veritas Truebreed, I've been to Kintucky and back—never you mind how, just let me tell you it wasn't easy and it was hardly what you might call a holiday excursion—and I've heard the whole sorry tale from the lips of Lewis Motley Wommack the 33rd his very own self, and you'd best hop it. Time's a-wasting."

The Magician of Rank stopped rubbing his hands together then, and blowing on them, and he leaned back against the stone of the tower, closed his eyes, and groaned aloud like a woman birthing.

"Only you could have brought this upon me, Troublesome of Brightwater," he said at last through clenched teeth, when he'd done with his groaning, "only you! We don't have trial and misery enough already; now we have to have *this*. Oh, for the power to do just one tiny Transformation. . . . I'd turn you into a slimeworm, with the greatest of pleasure, I'd step on you with my shoe heel . . . no, I'd set *fire* to you, right at the tender end where your little yellow eye was, and then—"

"Demented," said Troublesome.

"What?"

"You're demented. Mad. Plain crazy. And I've heard enough and a few buckets left over from you. I'm not *interested* in the twisted inventions of your imagination, Veritas Truebreed. I am interested in having you wake up my sister—bringing in all the other Magicians of Rank you need to help you at it, if that's required, and I suppose it is, though it's mighty curious that it takes nine-to-one odds for one small female like Responsible —and I'm interested in seeing if the Grannys are right that that will improve things around here a tad. Either you leave off your drivel and come along to get started on that, or I'll push you off the roof—how's that for managing without Formalisms & Transformations? Nothing fancy, O Mighty Magician, just shove you right off and let you try the effect of the stone down there in the courtyard on the very same body you came into this world with. You'll squash, I expect, and the Holy One knows you deserve it."

He opened his eyes and sighed, and she wondered impatiently what was next. There are only just so many meaningful noises in the sigh & moan & grunt & groan category, and he was running through them at a great rate.

"It can't be done," he said simply, and that surprised

96

her. "I'm more than willing, but it—cannot—be—done. Don't you think we *tried?*"

Troublesome hunched down beside him and regarded him seriously. This didn't look to be at all funny, if he spoke the truth.

"You explain," she said. "*Right* quick."

"When we realized what we'd done," said the man, making vague hopeless gestures, "we tried right away to undo it. The Mules weren't making more than about ten miles an hour by then, some of the boats were a knot or two faster, whatever was left of the energy that had been fueling the system was winding down fast . . . but since it had taken all nine of us to put Responsible into pseudocoma we had a feeling it would take all nine to get her back out again. We all got here; and since you were yammering about the difficulties of your jaunt to Kintucky, allow me to observe that there was nothing easy about *that*—but we did get here somehow. And in the dead of night we stood round her bed and we did everything we knew, and made up a sizable amount of stuff that had never been tried before . . . and we kept at it until there was barely time for some of us to get out before people saw us leaving. Whether everyone got back home again, I don't know . . . and I'm not sure I care. But we *did try*, Troublesome."

"And what happened?"

"And nothing happened. The only difference between pseudocoma and real coma is that the victim of pseudocoma does not deteriorate physically or mentally. Otherwise, it's exactly the same—and we did a good job of it. Oh yes; that's a downright magnificent pseudocoma we put her into. She went right on just as she was."

"Do you understand it?" Troublesome asked gravely.

"No, of course we don't understand it, curse your insolence for asking! We *ought* to understand it . . . do you have to rub my nose in it? Does that give you pleasure?"

"That's my sister," she reminded him. It was no time to make her ritual speech about having no human feelings.

"And the hope of the world."

To her amazement, she saw that there were tears on his cheeks, running in rivulets down into his beard; it wouldn't do to let him know she saw that, and she devoted her attention to watching a seabird wheeling above them. It must have gone demented, too, she thought absently.

"We were so careful," he mourned beside her. "One thousand years of being so *careful*. Keeping the population small, so that there was always abundance. Balancing every substance that went into the soil and the water and the air, and every substance that came out, to guard its purity. We made a paradise . . . no crime, no war, no disease, no crowding, no hunger, no—"

"I remember, Veritas Truebreed," Troublesome cut him off. "I was up on a mountaintop a good deal of the time, but I do remember. And I'd rather hear explanations than memorial services, if you don't mind."

"We have some guesses."

"Guesses? What kind of guesses?"

He didn't answer her, and she turned to look at him, tears or no tears.

"I said, what *kind* of guesses?"

"They ought, by rights, to be secret. . . ."

"Oh, hogwallow, you fool man! Secrets, at a time like this!"

"Maybe you're right," he said, "and I'm too tired to care any more . . . and nobody'd believe you even if you weren't too mean to tell, so what does it matter? We assume—just assume, mind you, we've no proof—that there was something about Responsible that was essential to the functioning of magic. She had no *powers*, of course, beyond those of any other female; don't misunderstand me."

"You're a liar, Veritas—I told you I had the whole story from that poor piece of work at Castle Wommack, and he had a few words to say about Responsible's powers; seems as how he mightily disliked being subjected to them."

"Even on Old Earth," said the Magician of Rank stiffly, "in the times of utter ignorance of magic, there were rare individuals capable of mindspeech—as there were rare individuals seven feet tall. Your sister is a freak, as those were freaks, with no knowledge or control of her abilities. But she is something else, something . . . a catalyst, perhaps? Somehow, whatever she was, taking her out of the system of magic brought it to a full stop. And pseudocoma *takes* magic—you can't put someone into it, nor take them out of it, with solar energy or electrical energy or any other kind. By the time

99

we realized what had happened, there was no energy lef
—without her—for us to use to cancel the coma. So fai
as I know, that's the way of it. And if you could get al
nine of us together in her bedroom again, which I
doubt, since the ships aren't sailing and the Mules
aren't flying, it would be the same as it was. Just the
same as it was. . . ."

"You were fools," said Troublesome. "Plain fools."

That long groan again . . . it was getting boring, especially since he was in no pain.

"You were, you know," she said, happy to twist the
knife.

"We didn't *realize*," he protested. "We had no idea
that she mattered that way. . . ." And if someone had
told them, he thought to himself, if they'd been warned,
it would have changed nothing. They wouldn't have
believed it. They had hated Responsible of Brightwater
so much, and they had so welcomed a legitimate opportunity to punish her for humiliating them, he knew that
no amount of warning could have held them back.

"You do not know the hours," he said slowly, "the
countless hours I have spent standing beside her all by
myself . . . trying things. Hoping I'd jog something
loose, find the right thread accidentally. Because whatever it is that she is for, *that* is still intact. *That's* still
there, if I could only get at it."

"How do you know that? How can you possibly
know?"

He raised his eyebrows at that, and he admonished
her to think. After all, he pointed out, she had a reputation for wisdom as well as wickedness. And, goaded like

that and held in the fierceness of his eyes wanting to get back at her for the way she'd spoken to him, she saw it.

"Ah," she breathed, "you're right! Otherwise, if it were *otherwise*, she'd be like someone in true coma . . . she'd be curled tight and wasting away and—"

"And all the rest of it. Yes. And she's not. She looks exactly as she looked the hour we did our work, and that can mean only one thing—all that is left of the energy of magic is concentrated there in her, keeping her from ever changing."

Something in his tone caught her attention, and she looked at him close, and marveled at the way of the world. Revelation followed upon revelation.

"You hate her," she said. "She's your own kin, grew up here under this roof playing on your knee and riding piggyback on your shoulders—and you hate her worse than sin! Why?"

Veritas Truebreed squared his shoulders, and he met her eyes, but he said not one word. No one not a Magician of Rank was ever going to know the answer to that question, not from his lips. Not ever.

"It must have been hard," murmured Troublesome. "All those years, pretending to be helpful . . . playing at being loyal."

"It was."

Troublesome went back down into the Castle, her breath making little white puffs in the air, and she found Grannys Hazelbide and Gableframe, and told them.

"It seems," she wound it up, "that you went through

all of this and gave up the last of your treasure things—
not to mention a certain amount of discommodance on
*my* part—all for nothing. It's a shame."

"No," said Granny Gableframe firmly. "It wasn't for
nothing, young woman. In *no* sense of the word. We
traded an ignorance big as this Castle for a whole *pot* of
knowledge, bubbling and simmering this minute. I'd say
as it was a fair trade. We're not out of it, mind you, not
by many a mile, but we at least know how we came to
be where we are."

"Knowledge," said Granny Hazelbide, "is for using.
Now we have some, the problem is how we put it to use.
And for that, Troublesome, we don't need you. No call
whatsoever to keep you from your homeplace any
longer, and we're grateful to you for what you've done,
however much it sticks in my craw to say it. We're beholden to you."

"Hazelbide, you exaggerate," said Granny Gableframe.

"You know any other living soul on this earth as
would of done what Troublesome did?" demanded
Granny Hazelbide. "Gone off in the cold and damp in a
leaky boat with a bribed crew, on what was ninety-nine-
to-one a wild goose chase? Gone off and chanced being
stranded forever in a wilderness, dying all alone in some
Kintucky briartangle? Just because we asked her to, and
no other compensation offered?"

"Flumdiddle!" said Gableframe. "The fact you raised
Troublesome's addled your brain—*which* it can't tolerate much of, I might add. That's her own sister as lies in
there, and it's her own people as are suffering. She had

as much to gain from this as any of us, and more than some, and I'll be benastied before I'll say we're beholden to Troublesome of Brightwater! The *idea!*"

"One more time, Gableframe," said Granny Hazelbide, tight-lipped. "Just *one more* time, I'll tell you. . . . Troublesome has no natural feelings. Responsible could die this minute, putrify right there on her bed, and her sister's only complaint'd be the smell. And that goes for every sick baby and hungry tadling and suffering human on the face of this world, you have my word on it. If *she* helped us, we're beholden. You care to be benastied as well, that's your choice."

Troublesome chuckled, and Granny Hazelbide said: "See there?"

They were sitting there together, the two old women rocking quick and hard to show their irritation, and Troublesome still grinning, when the Mules began to bray in the stables, and Granny Gableframe said, "There's somebody coming—listen to that racket!"

"Probably Lewis Motley Wommack the 33rd," observed Granny Hazelbide. "Swam all the way here for penance, and crawled the rest of the way when he ran out of water."

"For sure it's a strange Mule to bring all that on," said Granny Hazelbide. "That's all we need now, when we should be setting our minds to how to use what we've learned—company. Botheration!"

"Don't you get awfully tired of that?" asked Troublesome.

"Tired of what?"

"The formspeech. Having to go 'botheration' and 'I

swan' and 'flumdiddle' and 'mark my word' and all the rest of it. Do you keep it up when you're all by yourselves and nobody around to say, '*Eek!* I heard a Granny talking normal talk like anybody else'?"

The Grannys drew themselves up in outrage, right together like they'd practiced it, and Troublesome chuckled some more. There was nothing more fun to tease than a Granny.

"Troublesome of Brightwater," said Granny Hazelbide stiffly, "just you go and see who's come—or *what's* come, might could be that's more near the mark! I wish to goodness it *would* be young Wommack, I'd pull every hair of his beard out one at a time . . . but we'll not be that lucky, it'll be somebody useless, or worse. You've had your thanks, missy, and we've had your sass, and now we're even—make your young bones useful and see what's come to pass."

But Troublesome didn't have a chance to more than straighten up from her chair before a knock came at the door; and when they called, "Come in!" it was a servingmaid of Brightwater and an Attendant from Castle McDaniels, the latter looking as if he'd fall over if you blew on him.

"I'm here," he blurted out, "with a message for Miss Troublesome. Law, but I was scared to death she'd be gone before I got here. . . . Miss Troublesome, I'm pleasured to see you."

"First time in her life she ever heard *that!*" said the two Grannys together, and Troublesome allowed that it was, and the young man hurried to explain himself.

"I don't mean as how I'm happy to see *her*," he said

hastily, stumbling into the doorframe and causing the servingmaid to put a sturdy hand to his elbow to help him out. "Don't misunderstand me; it's that I'm happy to see she's not *gone* yet. If you see what I mean."

"The distinction's a mite subtle," said Granny Gableframe. "But we won't hold it against you, whatever it might mean, seeing as how it's clear you've had a hard ride and a long one and can scarcely stand on your feet, much less orate and do declamations. What are you after with Troublesome of Brightwater, young man?"

"Message from Castle McDaniels, ma'am," he said, bobbing his head. "And it's urgent."

"Then de*liver* it," snapped Troublesome, running out of patience. "*Before* you fall over. It'll be more practical that way, by a good deal. And don't mumble. When I get urgent messages brought in to me at a last gasp like this I like them to be turned over with *clarity*."

"Troublesome!" Granny Hazelbide was fairly quivering. "*Will* you not tease the poor young man, for all our sakes!"

"Oh, that's all right, Granny Hazelbide," said the Attendant from McDaniels, trying not to lean on the servingmaid. "I've been warned about her already, at some length. Missus McDaniels, her that was Anne of Brightwater, she talked to me about Miss Troublesome for it must of been a good hour and a half. I expected horns and a tail on her, if you want to know the truth of it."

And Troublesome chuckled some more. For a day that had begun with spoiled food and bad water and a crew of sick and surly men on a leaky boat, this one was turning out to have its good parts.

"Well, then," she said. "You've seen me, and you're disappointed I don't live up to your expectations. That's clear. Now pass on the message, and you can be on your way and get some rest. Just speak right up."

"You're to stay here," said the Attendant.

"I'm to stay here? That's it? That's your urgent message?"

"Because Miss Silverweb's coming," he told her. "She wasn't quite ready to leave when I was, and she couldn't of kept up with with me if she had been, I'm sure—I was told to ride hard all the way and not spare the Mule or me either one. But she says you're to stay right here until she gets here, never mind how anxious you are to leave, and never mind how much there's people encouraging you on your way."

"Miss Silverweb said that?"

"Yes, miss. And her mother as well."

"Hmmmph."

Troublesome gnawed on her braid, and the Grannys stopped their rocking, and Granny Hazelbide pointed out that considering the number of days she'd lost already another one couldn't do much harm. Or another two.

"Did she say *why*?" Troublesome asked the Attendant.

"Miss?"

"Did either of those women say *why* I was to wait?" asked Troublesome impatiently. "I can't see much point to it myself—I don't even *know* Silverweb of McDaniels, except that I believe I changed one of her diapers

106

once. She for sure does not know *me*. Why should I wait for her?"

"Well," said the Attendant, "I can't say as I understand it. But I can tell you what they said to me."

"You do that, then," said Troublesome.

"Miss Silverweb, she said I was to tell you just this: you stay here, because she knows how to wake up Miss Responsible, but she needs your help to do it. And that's all."

The silence went on and on, and the Attendant leaned more and more obviously on the servingmaid, who fortunately showed no sign of collapsing under the strain, and when Troublesome spoke at last her voice was hesitant.

"You say that Silverweb of McDaniels knows how to wake my sister. . . ."

"So she claims, miss. I'm just passing it on, as I was bid."

Troublesome turned to the Grannys.

"Well?" she asked them. "Is it likely? You know the girl . . . any reason she should know what nine Magicians of Rank *don't*?"

"Miss Silverweb'll be here by morning at the latest," pleaded the Attendant. "And if I've got here and told you, and you're gone on anyway, I won't dare go back, I can tell you. Missus Anne was *most* particular about that. 'If she doesn't wait for Miss Silverweb, don't you bother coming back here,' she said to me. And I've worked there, and done my job *right*, more'n six years now. Shows where hard work won't get you."

## And Then There'll Be Fireworks

"Troublesome," said Granny Gableframe, speaking right up, "I can't say honestly I know any reason why you should stay. Rumor is, Silverweb of McDaniels' gone some kind of religious lunatic, shut up all the time in an attic praying and carrying on. Not that I don't hold with prayer, mind you, indeed I do, in its place— but they say Silverweb carries it to and beyond extremes. On the other hand, reason or no, what's the harm? What's one more day to you? You've got no appointments to keep on your mountain, what's a few hours more or less at Brightwater?"

Troublesome gave it a minute or two for real, and a minute or two for tormenting them, and then she nodded slowly, and the Attendant went limp with relief and very nearly did fall down.

"All right," said Troublesome. "I don't suppose it can make any difference; and I don't mind admitting I'm curious. I'll wait for the child. Pray with her if need be."

"She's no child, Miss Troublesome," said the Attendant, very serious in spite of his exhaustion. "You wait till you see her—that's no child, nor ever will be again. Nor no woman, either."

"Well, what is she, then?"

"You'd best wait and see for yourself," the Attendant said, and that appearing to be all he could manage, the Grannys motioned for the servingmaid to take him away. Which she did, murmuring soothing words to him all the way down the corridor.

"Youall don't know anything about this?" demanded Troublesome, arms akimbo. "This is no Granny mischief, cooked up between you?"

"Honestly," said Gableframe. "How you talk."

"Your word on it or off I go this minute," declared Troublesome.

"Phooey," said Granny Gableframe right back at her. "It'll be a fine day when I give you my word on anything. As soon give my word to my elbow. And who are *you* to doubt a Granny's word?"

"Troublesome," put in Granny Hazelbide hastily, "I'm with Gableframe on that. But you said you'd stay. And you know this is no scheme we planned for you— we've got no heart these days for schemes. Leave off your nonsense, now, and keep *your* word."

"And so I will," said Troublesome. "I beg your pardon, I forget sometimes the way things have changed in this world. Up on that mountain . . . I don't see it the way youall have to."

"Understandable," said Granny Gableframe. "Not natural; but understandable."

"I suppose they'll make me sleep in the stable," Troublesome fussed.

"I'll put you up in my own room if they try it," said Granny Hazelbide. "I'm not afraid of you, and the Twelve Gates knows I'm *used* to you."

"I'd rather stay in the stable."

"Suit yourself. Just so's you stay."

"*My* word on it, to you and to my elbow," said Troublesome solemnly, crossing her heart elaborately with one finger. "I'll wait for little Silverweb and see what she's got to offer."

# CHAPTER 7

There was no order to it, when it happened—it happened everywhere, all at once, all at the same time. Twelve Castles there were on Ozark, and not one was overlooked or granted a delay. Nine Magicians of Rank as well, spread around over the planet, and they were stricken all together, with a unity that they had known before only on that single occasion when they had joined forces against Responsible of Brightwater.

Veritas Truebreed Motley the 4th was the only Magician of Rank on the continent of Marktwain, and the course of events was so swift that he heard only the first scream from outside the Castle walls before he was literally thrown to the floor with his hands pressed desperately to a head that he was sure would burst . . . he could hear nothing more after that but the message exploding there.

The ordinary citizens and the Grannys were spared that penalty; the Magicians felt only a sudden nagging headache, nothing out of the way. For them, unlike the Magicians of Rank, the problem was not what was in their heads but what was in the sky.

Above Castle Brightwater, suspended well out of reach of ordinary weapons but easily within sight of the eye, a giant crystal had appeared, spinning slowly on its point for just a moment before it stopped and hung there motionless above them.

It looked to be one hundred feet from tip to tip, stretching straight up, though it was hard to be sure without knowing exactly what its distance was from any object of reference. And it was in the shape of a flawless diamond, perfect in its symmetry, perfect in its utter transparentness. It would have been invisible, in fact, except that from some angles it acted as a prism and cast huge rainbows over the land and buildings beneath it, turning the countryside to a fairyland of glorious color. It made no sound at all. It came from nowhere and nothing held it in its place, nothing that could be seen. It was beautiful, and mysterious, and wholly terrifying.

The Grannys heard the screaming and ran out onto a balcony to see what the commotion was about *this* time, took one horrified look at the thing, and ran even faster after Veritas Truebreed. By the time they reached him he was aware that similar scenes were taking place at every one of the Twelve Castles, and he wished himself anywhere else in the Universe . . . preferably at the bottom of the sea. Any sea.

"Veritas Truebreed Motley," fussed Granny Gableframe when they found him, "whatever in this world are you doing? A lot of help *you* are, rolling on the floor and carrying on with that carry-on! You have colic or what? Get up and come see what's arrived this day to brighten the corners where we are . . . might could be you could be of some use at last!"

When that didn't budge him from the niche he had

managed to thrash his way into, or bring him out of the position of tight-coiled agony he was twisted into, the Grannys knelt beside him and began an expert probing. He screamed louder, and begged them not to touch him, and if he had not been paralyzed with pain they would not have been able to stop his frenzied efforts to smash his brains out against the stone walls of the Castle.

"Men," said Gableframe. "Always there when you need them."

"Veritas?" Granny Hazelbide stood up and poked him with her shoe. "You stop that caterwauling, you hear me? I know you can hear me, don't you make out you can't!"

As a matter of actual fact, he could *not* hear her over the din in his head. He could see her mouth moving, and his long experience with Grannys gave him an excellent idea of what the two of them must be saying, but they might as well have been in the next county for all that he was able to hear of their bad-mouthing. There was only *one* sound, and it filled all his perceptions, and it was surely going to be the death of him unless he somehow got help. He had time to wonder, through his agony, how Lincoln Parradyne was faring at Castle Smith, where the "Granny" in residence was only an old woman hired by the Magician of Rank to placate the Family when Granny Gableframe walked out on them to move to Castle Brightwater. Veritas Truebreed had sense enough left to know that nobody but a Granny was likely to be able to help any of them.

*One word, Veritas,* he was screaming at himself silently, trying to get through the unbearable waves of noise, *you've got to say one word! Only one word!*

Granny Hazelbide poked at him again disgustedly with the tip of one pointy-toed black high-heeled shoe, and was just getting ready to draw back her foot for an actual kick when he finally succeeded in croaking out that word. And it brought both old women to rigid attention as if it had been a Charm and a Spell and a Transformation all combined into one. The sound that had come out of Veritas' mouth, strangled and deformed but comprehensible, was the word "Mules!" And once again, before he went back to the howling that was completely unlike the cries from outside— those were only terror—he said it: *"Mules!"*

"Mules," repeated the Grannys, looking at one another. "Do you suppose . . ."

"I do," said Granny Gableframe. "What else could do that?"

"Maybe that thing hanging over our heads," said Granny Hazelbide grimly, pointing up at the ceiling and tapping her foot to a smart beat. "Two sharp ends it's got like a double needle, and no knowing what it can do."

"Well, we can't talk to *it*, Hazelbide," snorted Granny Gableframe, "that's for sure. And the Twelve Gates only knows what will happen if one of those scared sick lunatics out there takes it into his head to shoot at the thing with a laser . . . likely to mean the end of all of us, and nothing left where Ozark was but a

114

puff of dust, if that happens. The Mules, on the other hand, we could talk to."

"Gableframe . . ."

"I said *talk* to! Not either one of us is equipped to do any mindspeaking, and the Mules know that full well. I mean *talk*, ordinary tongue-and-mouth-and-teeth talk."

"What makes you think they'll listen?"

"Hazelbide, you have brains in that head or pudding?" Granny Gableframe was clear out of temper. "Stand there and go wurra-wurra like that poor fool on the floor if you like, but any ninny can see there's no way of talking to that . . . creation . . . up in the air, and the only clue we've got is what Veritas said, and I intend to hightail it for the stables!"

Granny Hazelbide knew sense when she heard it; she followed the other without a word, and without a glance behind her for the Magician of Rank in his awesome misery. She was only sorry there wasn't time to look for Troublesome and make her go along with them.

At the stables, they found the Mules standing in ominous silence. If the expressions on their faces could be interpreted in any human framework, they looked both grim and determined. In any framework, they had their attention fully occupied with something.

Granny Gableframe marched up to Sterling, the best creature in the stable, and said howdydo and she'd like it to listen to her. And when that had no effect, she whacked it smartly right between the eyes.

"You, Mule!" said Gableframe. "I want a word with

you, and I *do* know that you can understand me just fine!"

Sterling rolled her eyes and laid back her ears, and Granny Gableframe whacked her again. She'd never thought to see the day she'd be dealing with a hysterical *Mule.*

"You want to listen polite-like and of your own free will, that's fine with me," said the old lady. "I'll be polite, too, as is proper; it pleasures me not atall to abuse any creature. But if you'd rather do it the hard way, I'm prepared for that, and I *do* intend to have you hear me."

"You think that'll work?" asked Granny Hazelbide, tapping her nose with her pointing finger. "It was always Responsible as talked to the Mules, and she had a mighty different approach to it."

"You have a better idea?"

"No-sir, you go right to it. And I'll try another one," said Granny Hazelbide, and went off to make her word good.

"Sterling," said Granny Gableframe, "I have reason to believe you're trying to mindspeak poor Veritas Truebreed, and I'm here to tell you that if that's what you're up to you're pouring sand down a rathole. He's curled up in a hole in the wall like a puking babe, howling and begging to be shot or poisoned a one, he doesn't care which, and a less promising mode of communicating I've never come across in all my born days! Now if you have something you'd like to get across to the Magician of Rank, m'dear Mule, I'd suggest you turn down the power somewhat more than a tad. You are addressing a

uman male, not Responsible of Brightwater, and he is
ost surely not up to taking in what you are putting
ut. Do you hear me, Sterling?"

The Mule gave her a look down its nose, and raised
s ears one notch, and the Granny said it all over again,
ith more emphasis in the hard places.

"Tone it down!" she admonished Sterling, winding it
p. "Tone it down or you might as well leave off en-
rely! That man's mind is frail as a flower petal up
ere, you can't just go banging around in it like some
ind of natural disaster!"

Sterling whickered and ducked her head, and the
ules all around joined in.

"You suppose, Granny Hazelbide," said Gableframe
en, out of breath entirely, "you suppose that means
e got it across?"

"If we didn't, we probably can't," came the answer,
and the only way I know to find out is to go see what's
ft of old Veritas Truebreed." She brushed down her
kirts and sneezed twice at the dust and remarked on
ablemaids and how they got lazier every year, and
ableframe did the same, and then they looked at each
ther.

"You ready?" said Hazelbide.

"I'm not ready to go out and walk under that *thing*
anging in the air over my head; nor am I ready to see
very last soul running around and screaming like their
ils was caught in a door when it hasn't yet done any of
m ary harm *what*soever . . . and I for sure don't want
go stare at that pitiful excuse for a Magician of *Rank*.
ut I will, Hazelbide, I will. Let's get at it."

117

"Fool Mules," Granny Hazelbide grumbled. "Now what?"

And all the way back to the Castle door and up the steps, she grumbled. It was one thing for the Mules to mindspeak the Magician of Rank—the Magicians had always known the Mules were telepathic, and vice versa —but the *Grannys* weren't supposed to know all that. But Granny Hazelbide was ready to bet twelve dollars to a dillyblow that when the Mules *did* turn down their power of projection to accommodate the limitations of Veritas Truebreed's mind the very first thing they'd done was inform him that the Grannys had told them to do so. And *that* was going to be a fine kettle of fish.

Things were a mite less chaotic . . . the townspeople had recovered from their first shock at the sight of the giant crystal and were gathered in clumps, talking and shaking their heads. This was not exactly the normal order of the day, but the Grannys found it an improvement on the original running around in circles and screaming. They hurried past a group of Attendants and servingmaids that looked ready to head them off, and went straight on up to Veritas Truebreed to see if their trip to the stables had been a mission of mercy or a red herring.

They found the Magician of Rank much the worse for wear, white as a sheet and soaked with cold sweat, still rubbing his head and trembling all over. But he was able to talk.

"According to the Mules," he said gruffly when they came through his door, "I've you to thank for an end to

118

that unspeakable torture. And I *will* thank you—
because if it had not stopped I would be dead—and
then I would appreciate an explanation."

Granny Gableframe didn't miss a beat. She reminded
him that the Mules' telepathic ability was a pretty open
secret after all these years. And she reminded him that
*he* had been the one bellowing "Mules!" and they'd
only followed directions. "And as for mindspeech," she
finished up crisply, "we Grannys don't have it, so you
needn't go searching for revelations there. We went
down to the stable and whacked the Mules over the
head and told them—out loud—that if they were trying
to talk to you they were hollering themselves into obliv-
ion . . . and then we came back to see what happened.
You appear to be recovered—"

"I will *never* be recovered from that, thank you very
much!"

"Never mind, Veritas Truebreed, you are at least on
your feet and talking 'stead of howling, and we'll accept
that for now. The question is: what have the Mules
been telling you?"

The Magician of Rank swallowed and stammered,
and Granny Gableframe threatened to kick him with
her shoe the way Granny Hazelbide had.

"Speak up," she said, infuriated. "Time's a-wasting!
The Mules never tried mindspeaking you before, and
there's never been a gigantic humungus *bo*dacious
chandelier-bobble hanging up in the air before, and I for
one am inclined to believe there's got to be a connection! What did the Mules want with you?"

"It's a wild tale," said Veritas Truebreed.

"It's a wild *sight*," said Granny Hazelbide. "You take a look?"

"I looked. I saw . . . it. One of the basic primordial shapes."

"Primordial shapes be hanged, do you know anything *use*ful?"

"Careful, Hazelbide, you'll have a heart attack," cautioned Granny Gableframe. "And a lot of help that'll be."

"Well, the man's *mad*dening!"

"And if I had four wheels I'd be a tin lizzy. Calm down and let him talk . . . he'll get around to it. Eventually."

He did.

"It seems," he said slowly, "according to the Mules, it seems that thing you refer to as a chandelier-bobble is a kind of mechanism for the focusing of energy. It pulls in energy and concentrates it . . . and stores it."

"To do what with?"

"Just a minute. . . ." Veritas Truebreed wiped his brow with the back of a shaking hand. "I've got to sit down."

Granny Gableframe clucked her tongue and told him not to be such a sissy, but he sat down all the same.

"The Mules tell me," he said when he was settled, "that there is a group of planets not too far away from here that is called the Garnet Ring; and that their representatives—something called the Out-Cabal, and according to the Mules you'll be able to fill me in on that, and I will assuredly be interested in knowing *why*

—that their representatives have been keeping an eye on us for some time. The crystal out there is sent by the Garnet Ring, on the basis of information reported back by this . . . Out-Cabal . . . and the Mules say there's one just like it over each of the Castles of Ozark."

"Ohhhh dear!" cried Granny Hazelbide. "Oh my! That is a predicament, for sure and for certain!"

"Indeed it is," echoed Granny Gableframe. "They tell you anything more, Veritas Truebreed?"

"I got the distinct impression," he snapped at her, "that you two knew more about this than they did."

"Not accurate," said Gableframe. "Not precisely."

"*Isn't* it? According to the Mules—"

"You believe a passel of pack animals, Veritas, or you believe two respectable Ozark Grannys?"

"After what they did to me? Those 'pack animals' you mention? I believe *them!*" The Magician of Rank was furious, and beginning to feel more himself. "It's more than clear that some very important information has been kept from the Magicians of Rank by the Grannys of Ozark for hundreds of years—information that might well have been crucial to the running of this planet— and I want you to know that I resent it, and that *steps will be taken!*"

"You don't say?" Granny Gableframe said. "What do you have in what's left of your mind, Mister High-andmighty? You without so much as a Housekeeping Spell on hand! You get your powers back . . . such as they were, such *as they* were . . . and then you can prattle about taking steps. In the meantime, you mind your mouth."

"*You* are an unpleasant old woman," said the Magician of Rank.

"Grannys are supposed to be unpleasant old women," retorted Gableframe. "You want something young and willing, you don't go looking for a Granny. Now what I'd like to know is how long that thing's going to be a part of our sky out there and what it's intended to do to us. If you know, we'd appreciate you spitting it out."

And then she muttered, "Oh, law, it heard me!" as a sudden pulsing . . . not exactly a sound, more a kind of powerful vibration that thrummed in the stone walls and floors . . . began. "I suppose that's it, warming up," she said.

"I suppose so too," said Veritas Truebreed. "How would I know? Until this accursed day, I had never heard of an Out-Cabal. Nor a Garnet Ring. You ladies have minded *your* mouths admirably."

"It was our duty to do so," said Granny Gableframe. "Quit your complaining over things you admit you don't know any more about than the doorknob does."

"The Mules say," Veritas Truebreed sighed, "that this planet is about to be taken over by the Garnet Ring. We are, they tell me, now 'eligible'—that's the way they put it—to be so treated. The crystals will remain where they are, doing whatever that is they're doing, until they are fully charged. And then, I am assured, we will be unable to resist this Garnet Ring. And I suppose it's true?"

"Could we do anything like those crystals?" asked the Grannys in one voice.

"They might could be only an illusion," added

Granny Hazelbide. "I've seen you Magicians of Rank do some fancy things along that line, in my time."

Veritas Truebreed shook his head. "The Mules tell me they're real, and that they're as powerful as the Out-Cabal says they are, and that they can do what they claim. Now *you* tell *me* if the Mules are likely to know what they're talking about."

"Well, it's misery," said Granny Gableframe, "just plain misery—but we have no reason to think they don't. And plenty to think they do."

"Then we know where we are," he said wearily.

"Do we know how much time we have?"

"We have whatever time it takes until those things are 'fully charged,' like I said before. That's all the Mules knew."

"Well," asked Granny Hazelbide, "what do you plan to do?"

"Me? I plan to go lie down and not move my head until the Out-Cabal comes to cut it off."

"My, *that's* impressive!" scoffed the Granny. "You expect a medal for that, do you?"

"Be reasonable!" shouted the Magician of Rank, and winced at what it did to his aching head. "As you so politely pointed out to me, not three minutes ago, I haven't a Housekeeping Spell to my name. What do you *expect* me to do?"

"There are a lot of people out there," said the Granny, "as are frightened half to death. They're not as accustomed to wonders and marvels as you are, not by a long sight. And they respect you, magic or no magic. I'll thank you to go get on the comset and spread the word —in some suitable form. I don't believe I'd tell them what you just told us, not quite yet. Just get on there and tell them that there's no reason to be afeared right at this very minute, which is true. And that we'll get back to them, which is true. And that we're working on the problem—which is true. I do believe you could handle that, Veritas, and I believe you're obliged to. *Right* now!" She did not say scat, out of politeness.

On his way out the door, moving as fast as his condition would allow, and making other allowances for the unsteady feeling the whole Castle had with that low vibration running all through it, he very nearly ran right over Silverweb of McDaniels.

"Silverweb—" he began, but the Grannys, right behind him, gave him a push.

"Not *now*, Veritas Truebreed Motley, not *now!*" fussed Granny Hazelbide. "Whatever Silverweb of McDaniels needs, it won't be anything as concerns you, and you're needed to stop the panic out there in the town and all around the countryside. We Grannys'll see to Silverweb!"

But Silverweb needed no seeing to at all. She was as radiant as if she'd been living on strawberries and thick cream, as beautiful as ever, and as serene as if this were the most ordinary of days. She was there, she announced, to get Troublesome—and the Grannys realized they'd seen no sign of Troublesome of Brightwater through all of this, which was becoming of her and showed a proper consideration—and then Silverweb went on to say that she and Troublesome were going to take Responsible of Brightwater out into the desert of Marktwain to the sacred spring.

"We'll hitch a Mule to a wagon," said Silverweb, her voice like rich melted butter running over in the dish, "and spread it with a comforter and a pillow to make Responsible lie easy. And Troublesome and I will lay Responsible inside, and we will take her away."

"But, child," hazarded Granny Hazelbide, touching the arm of the creature—as the Attendant had said, not a child, and not precisely a woman, either, but the Granny had the privilege of her years—"this is no time for such a trek! Don't you know what's happened?"

"What has happened," said Silverweb of McDaniels, "is that the Holy One has spoken to me and told me that I must get Troublesome, and that she and I must take Responsible out into the desert. That is all that I need to know, Granny Hazelbide."

"But—"

"There's Troublesome now," added Silverweb. "Right on time."

Troublesome had her sister gathered up in her strong arms, a comforter wrapped round her, and no more trouble than a tadling; she wasn't even out of breath, despite all the stairs.

"You lead on, Silverweb," said Troublesome, "you're the one as knows how this is supposed to go. And I'll follow. Can you hitch up a Mule? If you can't, I can."

Silverweb laughed. "I can hitch a Mule," she said. "I

can hitch up any living thing that walks this planet, and I can do a sight more than that. You just come along with me—and I thank you kindly for waiting for me."

It took the Grannys' breaths away. They stood there in silence—not the usual way of things—as the two young women left with their sleeping charge. And then they watched from the balcony as the gates were opened and the wagon that carried Responsible was pulled out of the Castle yard by a prime Mule.

"That'll be Sterling," said Granny Hazelbide, and Granny Gableframe nodded.

"It would be."

"Whatever do you suppose is going to happen? There's nothing out there in that desert to eat nor to drink, and those two didn't gather up so much as a peachapple before they left here. . . ."

In the streets the people drew back, whispering under their breaths, to let the wagon through, and the parents held the tadlings up high to see. And above them, the crystal had lost its transparent clarity and was beginning to take on a pale garnet color, that pulsed along with the thrumming in the stone and in the air.

It was beginning to accumulate its charge.

# CHAPTER 8

Marktwain's desert, the one and only desert Ozark had, was something of a mystery. For one thing, the rest of the continent would have led you to believe there could be no desert there; Marktwain was lush green farming land, surpassed only by the emerald richness of Mizzurah, all the way to its coasts in all directions. That you could go through the pass between Troublesome's mountain and the others in its chain (not really much more than high hills, but the Ozark Mountains of Old Earth had not been towering peaks, either, and there was thus a precedent for it), and suddenly find yourself heading smack into a real desert—that was always a surprise.

It wasn't large, and was called simply "The Desert"; if you've only one, there's no special need to name it. The technology and the knowledge necessary to bind its sands with plant life and turn it green as the rest of the continent had been part of the Ozarkers' equipment even at First Landing. When Marktwain's population passed sixty thousand, the two Kingdoms of Brightwater and McDaniels all parceled out in towns and farms, the idea of keeping a desert for its unique character ceased to be anything but romanticism. But it was left alone, nevertheless, and it was a rare day when anybody did more than go to its border and glance out over its emptiness. The desert belonged, by treaty signed on First Landing, to the Skerrys.

Troublesome of Brightwater and Silverweb of McDaniels headed out into the desert, walking one on each side of the wagon, and the few people that had followed them that far turned back and let them go on. It was one thing to be those two and go trifling with the Skerrys; ordinary folk had best mind their own business.

And it was as well they did. Troublesome and Silverweb had hardly crossed the first smooth ridge of sand, talking idly of the foolishness going on in Smith Kingdom with its clown of a King and its dithery females, and on down the ridge's far side, before they saw ahead of them a group of Skerrys standing and waiting.

"How many do you think, Silverweb?" Troublesome asked softly, abandoning the ridiculous tale of the Smiths.

"I was told there would be forty-four," said Silverweb. "It is a number significant to them."

"Forty-four Skerrys!" Troublesome blew a long breath.

Not since First Landing had any Ozarker ever seen more than one Skerry at a time, and to sight one was so rare that it obligated the whole Kingdom where it happened to spend a day of celebration and full holiday in the Skerry's honor. Just what the sight of forty-four might have meant in the way of obligations was difficult to imagine. It surely would have been a heavy burden of worry and debate, and Marktwain's citizens had more than enough of worry on their plates at that moment.

Sterling stopped dead when *she* saw them, and would not take another step, and the two women hesitated, not sure whether to try forcing her on or not.

"What do you think, Silverweb?" Troublesome asked, measuring the animal with narrowed eyes. "Shall I encourage this blamed Mule a tad?"

Sterling's ears went flat back, and she walled her eyes, to indicate what she thought of the idea, but Troublesome was not impressed. "You care to find out who's meaner, you or me," she told the Mule, "I'm ready any time."

"I think I'd wait," said Silverweb, "and see if we get some kind of sign."

"Like forty-four Skerrys at once? Like a giant crystal over our heads?"

"I had something less outlandish in mind," Silverweb answered. For example . . ." And she pointed, doing it discreetly with the tip of her chin as befit a situation where the fine edges of manners weren't well known, toward the Skerry that had separated from the group and was heading toward them.

"Is it male or female, I wonder?" Troublesome said softly.

"We don't even know that there *are* male and female to the Skerrys," Silverweb reminded her. "We know only that they are more beautiful than anything else that we have ever seen."

And that was true. The one approaching them, moving over the sand with a gliding step like someone on ice, and at ease on ice, was blinding in its beauty. Much taller than Troublesome, who missed six feet by only a quarter of an inch, copper-skinned and its silver hair like a fall of water in the sun well below its waist, with eyes of purest turquoise, it lacked only wings to make it Angel. Angel of *what* was the question . . . and nobody knew.

As nobody knew what substance of bone must be required to support the slender muscular bodies of a race that claimed eight feet as its *average* height. Or how many there were, or what they ate, or why it was they hated all water except the narrow trickle they held sacred.

Another time, Troublesome would have been adding up the bits of data, storing them in her mind to puzzle over later, as she did faced with any mystery. But not now . . . not when the Skerry smiled at them, leaned over the wagon, and lifted Responsible up in its arms and against its slender body, leaving the comforters and pillows behind in the bottom of the wagon; and then it turned, motioning with its head for them to follow.

Troublesome didn't like that at all, and it distracted her attention completely. That was, after all, her own kin being galloped off with by a being that nobody knew whether it might eat her alive or keep her for a pet or skin her for her hide. But she hadn't much choice, either, distracted or not; they were outnumbered many times over, even if they'd known what manner of living thing they dealt with . . . and they didn't.

The voice in her mind was gentle enough, but it was firm.

DAUGHTER OF BRIGHTWATER, YOU THAT ARE NAMED TROUBLESOME, it said, LEAVE THE MULE AND THE

WAGON WHERE THEY ARE, AND FOLLOW US. NO HARM
WILL COME TO YOUR SISTER OR TO ANY OF YOU—HOW
COULD YOU THINK SUCH A THING?

Troublesome was not accustomed to mindspeech,
and she didn't like *that*, either. Two of the indigenous
species of Marktwain were telepathic, then. It made
sense, when you thought about it . . . how else could
the treaties have been negotiated? For sure, First
Granny and the others had not landed speaking
"Skerry," nor would the Skerrys have been fluent in
Ozark English. She'd never thought about it before, and
it was only that she was so flustered that she thought of
it now. It kept her mind off the possibilities up ahead,
that she could in no way predict. But it was said that
when the Mules mindspoke anybody they nearly destroyed that person's mind in the process. The Skerry's
voice in her mind only made her think of bells, chiming.
Deep bells.

THAT IS HOW YOU TELL, came the voice again, and
she judged that there was laughter in it. THE DEEP
BELLS ARE THE MALES, THE MIDDLE ONES OUR FEMALES,
THE MIXED ONES THE SHEMALES, AND THE HIGH CHIMES
ARE OUR CHILDREN, WHO DID NOT COME ALONG WITH US
TODAY.

"Oh, now, that's not likely!" Troublesome protested
aloud. She was impressed, but she would push just so far
and no farther. She had no intention of just *thinking* at
anything, if it did stand eight feet tall.

YOU ARE QUITE RIGHT, said a different voice. IT IS A
CONFUSION OF TRANSLATION. MY FRIEND MEANS THAT
THAT IS HOW YOUR HUMAN MIND INTERPRETS OUR

COMMUNICATION. YOU HAVE BELLS AVAILABLE TO YOU AS A MODE OF PERCEPTION; WE MAKE USE OF THAT MODE, FOR ITS CONVENIENCE . . . OTHERWISE, YOU WOULD HEAR . . . UNPLEASING NOISES.

"Botheration," said Troublesome, and hurried her pace to keep up. Beside her, Silverweb called ahead to the Skerry.

"She is one that would prefer privacy of mind," said Silverweb. "You are distressing her with your invasions."

"I'd live through it," said Troublesome crossly. "I've lived through worse, and I don't need mollycoddling."

"There's no need for it," Silverweb answered. "I am here, and if they want to use mindspeech they can do it through me. I don't mind it."

"Not at all? Having your whole mind naked like that?"

Troublesome said it before she thought; and then she knew a deep shame, remembering the way she had lambasted Lewis Motley Wommack the 33rd for expressing a similar dislike. And he had had it to bear, if he spoke the truth, over months—not just a few moments, as she had. It might very well be different with another human, instead of this alien creature; nevertheless, she was ashamed. She had not known what it would be like, nor had she made any attempt to *imagine* it.

"Not a scrap," said Silverweb of McDaniels. "Anything in my mind, they are welcome to. My only problem is keeping up with youall in this sand—I'm not exactly short, but the rest of you are a good deal longer of leg than I'll ever be." She was silent a minute, and then nodded. "They tell me," she went on, "that it is absolutely necessary for us to hurry—that the crystals charge quickly and we have no time to spare."

All the Skerrys had in fact gotten far ahead of both the Ozark women, who had had no practice walking over dry sand and were floundering as much as they were stepping.

"If we don't hurry it up, Silverweb, I'll wager they'll just pick us up and carry us, too," fretted Troublesome, "like a couple of armloads of kindling. You fall down, I'll smack you, so help me."

"Your bark," observed Silverweb, "is much worse than your bite. Why *do* you go on like that?"

Troublesome had the usual answer ready. "I have a reputation to maintain." She needed it embroidered across her chest.

"Worked hard building it up, too, as I recall."

"Far too hard to throw it away now, in the middle of a desert."

Silverweb laughed, and stumbled, and hurried on as best she could. The Skerrys were leading them eastward, toward a line of rocks humped up on the horizon. Darkest gray, almost black, some of them *jet* black, against the sand. Where the sun struck them, rays of light split out like spears. It was hard on the eyes; what would it be like if this were not wintertime?

"The spring is there by those rocks," said Silverweb. "Or so I have been told." Her yellow hair was coming down from its usual elegant figure-eight of braid, something Troublesome had never seen happen before; she found that it worried her, and she stopped to coil the heavy weight of it back again, tuck in the stray ends, and anchor it firmly with the ironwood pins.

"Careful, Troublesome of Brightwater," Silverweb teased her. "It begins with tidying up a friend in the desert, and first thing you know you are seized with a lust for helping people and taking in stray tadlings."

"Nonsense—I just can't abide mess."

Silverweb only laughed at her. "That's Responsible's line, my friend," she said, "not yours. You should see yourself."

"Silverweb?"

"Yes?"

"What happens when we get there?"

"Whatever happens. Don't dawdle, Troublesome."

"It's farther than it looks."

"Save your breath, then!"

It was wise counsel; Troublesome hushed and concentrated on closing the gap between them and the rocks. And at last they were there, a few minutes behind the party of Skerrys.

When she saw what they were doing, she would have rushed forward to stop them, but Silverweb had a firm and astonishingly powerful grip on her arm, and the voice of a Skerry rang, equally firm, inside her head.

WE ARE SORRY, it said, TO BE DISCOURTEOUS . . . IF ONLY WE HAD MORE TIME, WE WOULD OBSERVE YOUR PREFERENCES, BUT THE CRYSTALS ARE GORGING ABOVE YOUR CITIES. THERE IS NO TIME LEFT FOR NICETIES. TROUBLESOME OF BIRGHTWATER, SILVERWEB OF MCDANIELS, THIS IS WHAT MUST BE DONE . . . PAY CLOSE ATTENTION, AND DO NOT FORGET ANYTHING THAT WE

TELL YOU. TROUBLESOME, YOU SEE THAT ROCK, THERE WHERE THE WATER OVRFLOWS ITS BASIN?

The rock. Where the water overflows. Where her sister now lay naked, her hair loose in the water and her head pillowed on another rock set gently under it, where the water bubbled up out of some hidden source and poured over the still and lovely body. So frail, she looked!

"I see it."

TAKE YOUR PLACE THERE, came the voice. WE SKERRYS WILL FORM A . . . YOU HAVE NO SEMANTIC CONSTRUCT FOR IT, IT IS A SHAPE OF POWER . . . HERE AROUND THE HOLY WATER. YOU ARE TO SIT BESIDE YOUR SISTER, ON THAT ROCK. SILVERWEB, YOU OF CASTLE MCDANIELS, YOU WILL KNEEL UPON THE SAND, AND YOU WILL CALL DOWN THE LOVE YOU HAVE LEARNED TO DRAW UPON. YOU WILL ASK THAT THE SLEEPER WAKE, SILVERWEB OF MCDANIELS, WHILE WE SKERRYS SING FOR YOU. PLEASE, TAKE YOUR PLACES!

"I'm dreaming this," said Troublesome, too worried to be anything but cross and rude, but she did as she was bid, and she went and settled herself on the boulder near Responsible's head. Behind her, she heard the soft hiss of movement, and she looked over her shoulder and saw Silverweb kneeling on the sand with her arms raised to the sky and her eyes already rapt, even in the scalding sunlight and the constant battering of rays struck from the rocks. The Skerrys had taken up positions that looked to her to lack pattern of any kind, but she was willing to believe it was a congruent shape for them. She was willing to believe almost anything.

135

And now they were going to sing.

And Silverweb was going to pray.

"But what am *I* supposed to do?" she asked hoarsely; there was sand in her throat. "Outside of keeping this child from drowning, that is."

SHE WILL NOT DROWN, came a voice Troublesome felt was new. Not that it mattered. Bells are bells. THE WATER IS NOT DEEP ENOUGH OR SWIFT ENOUGH. THAT IS NOT THE DANGER.

"Tell me, then!"

IF SILVERWEB OF MCDANIELS IS SUCCESSFUL, IF THINGS GO AS WE EXPECT THEM TO GO, THERE WILL BE . . . SUDDENLY, WITH NO WARNING . . . A KIND OF TEAR IN THE FABRIC OF THE UNIVERSE. AT THAT INSTANT, WE BELIEVE THAT YOUR SISTER WILL WAKE. AND AT THAT SAME INSTANT, THERE WILL BE A CHANCE FOR SOMETHING EVIL TO COME THROUGH THE TEAR WE HAVE MADE, SOMETHING THAT WAITS ALWAYS FOR JUST SUCH AN OPPORTUNITY, THROUGH AGES UPON AGES OF TIME. YOU ARE TO PREVENT THAT.

Troublesome felt terror in her somewhere; she would have sworn there was none left in her.

The voice went on, confident, urgent, soothing her.

YOUR ROLE HERE, THE ROLE FOR WHICH YOU HAVE BEEN LEARNING ALL YOUR LIFE LONG, IS TO RECOGNIZE THAT EVIL THING HOWEVER BEAUTIFULLY IT MAY BE DISGUISED, AND TO STOP IT FROM ENTERING THIS SPACE AND THIS TIME. THAT, TROUBLESOME OF BRIGHTWATER, IS WHAT YOU ARE FOR IN THIS WORLD—WE NEED AN EXPERT IN EVIL.

Troublesome felt the terror go, and in its place a fragment of knowledge, as of something forgotten long ago and now remembered for a fraction of time. From the breadth of that scrap of remembrance, she straightened and stared at the Skerry she thought was speaking.

"Silverweb!" she cried out, taut as a bowstring. "What about Silverweb? You know what you leave her open to?"

SILVERWEB OF MCDANIELS IS PROTECTED. THERE ARE FEW SHIELDS SO INDESTRUCTIBLE AS PURITY AND VALOR IN COMBINATION. SHOULD ANYTHING GET NEAR HER WITH STRENGTH ENOUGH TO PASS THOSE SHIELDS, WE ARE MORE THAN ABLE TO DEAL WITH IT—AND IT IS NOT LIKELY. BUT ALL OUR ATTENTION, AND ALL OF HERS, MUST BE FOCUSED ON A SINGLE POINT. YOU ARE THE ONLY ONE, TROUBLESOME, WHO CAN PROTECT YOUR SISTER. BE READY, NOW! DON'T WATCH US; WATCH THERE, CLOSE BY HER HEAD, WHERE THE ANCIENT EVIL WILL TRY ITS BEST TO BREAK THROUGH. . . . IT IS WEARY PAST BEARING OF LYING TRAPPED BENEATH THAT SACRED SPRING!

Troublesome understood that well enough; she turned and set her eyes to watch, holding her breath, her lower lip caught between her teeth and her strong hands at the ready for . . . whatever might come.

And the Skerrys sang.

It was not precisely music, as Troublesome understood music. Nothing to it of fiddle or dulcimer or guitar, nothing of melody or harmony either; not even rhythm. She could make no sense of it, but it rose over the sand and the rocks with an unmistakable power. It was a call to that same Source that Silverweb called upon, and it supported her call, bore it up and carried it on what must have been notes and chords, focused it as Troublesome strained her eyes for anything—

There it was! Lovely in the water, a rose that rocked gently on the surface of the clear water, a single perfect yellow rose the size of her two cupped hands, with a scent that was as seductive as wickedness ever had been in all of time. Troublesome would have known it anywhere. She had it instantly, before it could drift one inch closer to the sands that were its first goal, crushed between her palms, and all her muscles knotted as she struggled with a loathsome squirming Unknown desperately determined to make the world its territory for a change.

"Nasty piece of work that you are," shouted Troublesome of Brightwater, laughing and exultant, "begone to wherever you came from, crawl back in your hole, you're no match for me, nor ever could be! Squirm all you like, and foul me all you care to . . . not even *trained*, are you? Ah, you're a sorry excuse for a Holy Terror, let me tell you; I was expecting more of a challenge!"

Occupied as she was, she had no way of knowing that the long silver hair of the Skerrys, and the tunics they wore, were being whipped and buffeted in a wind against which—for all their lives spent in this desert—they could scarcely stand. Or that their singing was being choked by the clouds of sand that had turned the sky black above them. Or that around Silverweb, like a shield shaped to her body, there was a clear space where no wind blew and no sand whirled, and all was still; and where all was radiant with a clear golden light that was the same color the evilness had chosen as a strategy to deceive them. Even the stench as the thing lost its control of scent-of-rose and began to pour out the smell that was natural to it could not break the concentration that poured through Troublesome's hands as they gripped her adversary by what might have been its throat.

That adversary did not impress Troublesome, nor could it touch Silverweb; they were the two polarities that served to hold this timespace intact. But the Skerrys were mightily impressed, and they gave a great sigh of relief in Troublesome's mind, all the bells calling out together, as they saw the golden rose crushed and rubbed to a slime in her hands, and they felt the wind fall and saw the desert sky clear once again.

Troublesome bent to rub her arms clean in the sand —she had no least intention of fouling the sacred water with the vile stuff that covered her to the elbows. Scrupulously, she gathered each grain that might have been contaminated by it into a heap before her, and she scrabbled a hole in the sands and shoved those soiled grains into it and laid a flat heavy rock over the spot to mark it. And still she wondered if that would do it . . . might could be there were tiny suckers and cells that would leach out through the sand and make the sacred water a new poison in a Universe already copiously overendowed with poisons. She was hesitating, crouched over the flat rock that seemed a puny barrier against such harm, when she felt Silverweb touch her shoulder, and jumped, startled.

"The Skerrys say," Silverweb told her, "that it is en-

tirely dead, with nothing left that can exist in this world.
They say it is not like other deaths, where a substance
will recombine as it goes back to its original elements
and enter the cycle of life again—it is too alien. You are
not to worry, they say; you did what was required, and it
is over."

"Well, it wasn't *much*," said Troublesome. "I could
do that every day and twice on Sundays."

"They would be pleased if you were denied any such
opportunity," said Silverweb dryly. "That's a direct
quote."

"Direct as you can make it, I expect. Bells . . . what
kind of language might that be?"

"Troublesome?"

Troublesome looked at her, still shaking the sand off
her arms.

"Yes, Silverweb?"

"It worked."

"What?"

"I said—it worked. Look there, behind you."

Troublesome whirled, and had she not been careful
she might well have cried, and spoiled her image forevermore. In the silver of the water, Responsible's eyes
were open, and she was speaking her sister's name.

# CHAPTER 9

Over Castle Airy, the giant crystal was beginning to take on the color of the small mallows that grew wild along Oklahomah's seacliffs; a tinge redder than the pale color of peachapple cider well made, but not yet the color of strawberry wine. As the crystal's pulsing grew stronger, its humming more clearly felt somewhere in the marrow of the bones, the point that aimed toward the sky and the point that aimed straight down toward the Castle itself began to look as if they could pierce both targets. They were darker at the points.

The people of Airy had gone inside their houses, and were huddled with their families. If they were to die, they would at least die together, not alone out in a field or a stable, or back of a counter in some store, some workshop. It was better to wait with your children and your kin and whoever you might love close by you. There was no doubt in their minds that they were going to die.

They only wondered how it would be. Would the thing plunge down toward the ground like a missile and explode in rosy flame or rosy poison? A gas, perhaps, spreading out over the Kingdom and taking them all as it coursed the air? And would it be a merciful poison, one that meant no more than a kind of falling asleep?

141

Or would there be convulsions and agonies and desperate clawing at the throat? Or would it stay there in the air and send out its cargo of death in rays, as the lasers did? Or something else, something completely unknown . . . and would it be *merciful* . . . or would it be the stuff of nightmare? They looked at the tadlings, and especially at the babies, and prayed that it would be merciful, and swift.

At the Castle, Charity of Airy and the three Grannys in residence could feel the terror. It took no telepathic powers to sense an emotion like that, coming from every side of you, and they bit their lips and frowned till their heads ached. It wouldn't do to take the contagion of that terror; might could be they would be needed later, and in their right minds.

Castle Airy had no Magician of Rank for the Mules to contact; and given that there were three Grannys there to be put up with that was not surprising. But the word had come in from Brightwater by comset almost at once, Veritas Truebreed Motley passing it along just as calm as he would have announced a blizzard. The women of the Castle blessed the fortune that had made them part of that system, and wondered what it was like for the Kingdoms that were neither part of the Alliance of Democratic Republics nor supplied by a Magician of Rank . . . they would be completely isolated now.

Granny Forthright didn't like it a bit.

"That thing up there," she fussed, waving at the ceiling over her head with one knitting needle, "it scares the bejabbers out of me—and *I* know what it is, not to mention knowing that Airy's not the only Castle so blessed.

And Then There'll Be Fireworks

Now what do you suppose it must be like for the Families that *don't* know those things?"

"Well, it won't *do*," pronounced Granny Flyswift. "And that's all there is to it."

"I agree, it won't," said Charity of Airy, "but talk is cheap—I suggest we give it some careful thought before we go doing anything. Is there truly anywhere that there's neither comset transmission, nor Magician of Rank, nor even a friendly neighbor to pass the word along? Count them off, ladies, and carefully!"

"Brightwater, McDaniels, Clark, and Airy," said Flyswift. "All on the comset, all brought up to date by Veritas Truebreed. That's four."

"Mizzurah's got no comsets," put in Granny Heatherknit, "but there's a Magician of Rank at Castle Motley for the Mules to tell direct, and Granny Scrabble there to see to it they don't kill him in the process. And seeing as Mizzurah's not much bigger all told than our back garden, there'll be somebody on the way to Castle Lewis with a message long since. That's six. And Tinaseeh . . . bad cess to it anyway . . . Tinaseeh's got *four* Magicians of Rank at Castle Traveller, no need to worry about *that* crew. And Granny Leeward, which is a shame; I'd of been right pleased to see the four at Traveller get their brains scrambled."

"Granny," chided Charity of Airy. "How you talk!"

"That's seven," said Granny Heatherknit, ignoring her completely. "Seven of twelve."

"Castle Guthrie on Arkansaw has a Magician of Rank, and so's Castle Farson—that's nine . . . oh, law!" Granny Flyswift made a soft and sorrowful noise.

"Ah, law," she said, counting it up on her fingers, "it'll be Purdy and Wommack as think they're all alone in this. No comsets, no Magicians of Rank, no way to know whatever in the world is happening and nobody as would care to make the effort to tell them. I can't say as I'm specially worried about the Wommacks—"

"You should be," Granny Forthright interrupted. "They'll be declaring it's the Wommack Curse again."

"Forthright, that slipped my mind entirely! You're right as right! And wouldn't you know it, wouldn't you just *know* it, it'd be the fool Purdys, as don't know enough to come in out of the rain anyhow, and the Wommacks with their fool *curse*, as are left stranded?" Granny Flyswift raised a finger beside her eyeglasses. "It's near on enough to make a body think they may *have* something with their curses and their poor-mouthing about bad luck following 'em everywhere and everywhen!"

"They make their own luck," Charity of Airy scoffed, "and you know it—don't talk nonsense at a time like this! Anybody wants a curse bad enough can manage to bring one down; you just have to put your back into it. And there's nothing we can do about either Wommacks or Purdys—they might as well be back on Old Earth for all we can do."

"And that makes *eleven*," Granny Heatherknit pointed out. "There's somebody left out."

"That's easy done and easy accounted for," said Granny Heatherknit. "*Nobody* wants to think about the Smiths. The Purdys now, they just need encouragement and they'd be all right. And the Wommacks, a good

clout between the eyes'd break them of blaming everything and its little fingernail on their old curse. But the
*Smiths,* I declare there's no hope for them! Do you
know, they caught one of their Attendants *again*—this'll
be what, the ninth time?—trying to tap into the comset
transmissions in the dark of the night? I cannot *believe*
the—"

"Granny Heatherknit!" Charity of Airy so rarely
raised her voice that they all three jumped, and Heatherknit closed her mouth in sheer surprise. "If the whole
world came to an end in a thunderclap, you wouldn't
have time to get ready, for it would catch you gossip-
ing!"

"Begging your pardon, Charity," said Granny Heatherknit. "I got carried away."

"And I assume," Charity went on in a more normal
tone, "that we've no reason to concern ourselves with
the Smiths. They've got Lincoln Parradyne Smith the
39th over there, and whatever else he may be, he's a perfectly good Magician of Rank. It'll be only the Wommacks and the Purdys, poor souls."

"You don't suppose the Mules would call on the
Grannys in such a hardscrabble?" hazarded Flyswift.
"Castle Purdy has one, and there's two in residence at
Castle Wommack."

All four women shuddered at the very idea, and the
other two Grannys gave Flyswift a long hard look.

"If they did," said Granny Forthright solemnly,
"there's now three less Grannys on Ozark."

"Pshaw! I'm not so sure," said Flyswift. "No, I'm *not*
so sure as a Granny's mind is any punier than a Magi-

cian of Rank's. Who's to say, excepting always the Magicians of Rank theirselves, and why wouldn't they?"

"You care to try mindspeech with a Mule?" demanded Granny Heatherknit. "*Or* anything else as lives and breathes? Or doesn't, for that matter?"

Granny Flyswift admitted that she wouldn't, particularly.

"Well, then."

Charity of Airy, tucking back a strand of the hair now gone snow white with the long months of hardship and worry, made a sudden hushing sound. That was twice she'd caught them by surprise in one morning—it was not like Charity to be ill mannered—and they thought as they often had lately how she'd gone gaunt and old since pneumonia had taken her daughter Caroline-Ann. She'd doted on Caroline-Ann, had Charity.

"You thought of something, Charity?" asked Granny Heatherknit gently. "*Have* we forgotten somebody? Twelve Families there's always been, and twelve we've counted off—unless a thirteenth's landed, and a fine time they've picked if they have, I must say! We've accounted for all, to my mind."

"It's not that," said Charity. "No, it's something that just struck me. And I may not be right."

"And you may not be wrong, either. Many a long year now you've been solving problems, it stands to reason you'd get good at it," said Granny Heatherknit. "What's struck you, m'dear?"

"Those things. Those crystals."

"Struck us all, I do believe, Charity."

"Yes, but I've been thinking about them. . . ."

Veritas Truebreed Motley says they're devices to gather up energy, focus it—that they're up there charging, like batteries. And I ask myself, where are they *getting* that energy? It's happening fast, Grannys. You go look and see how much darker they are, and feel how much louder! What are they drawing on for a source?"

"Charity, might could be there's a mothership up there, beaming it down to them; might could be *any-thing!*"

The Grannys nodded, all in agreement on that; the unknown was, after all, the unknown. But Charity had something on her mind.

"I have an idea," she declared, "and I plan to spread it!" And she was running for Castle Airy's comset speaker, her skirts hitched up in one hand and the cane she'd taken to using lately clutched in the other.

"*If* I can get through!" she called back over her shoulder, and out the door she went, leaving the Grannys staring after her.

"Well," said Granny Heatherknit to the others, "better one of us turn on the set over there or we'll miss it ourselves, and wouldn't *that* be a comedown? Not a one of us as can keep up with Charity, cane or no cane."

Granny Flyswift moved slowly, belying her name, but she was close by the comset stud, and it flickered and came on about three words into Charity of Airy's message.

"—to me," she was saying. "I might could be wrong, but I have a feeling about this. The crystals over the Castles, they're nothing more than enormous batteries, *storage* cells, and till they're charged they can't harm us.

nd perhaps they charge on sunshine, or wind, or
tardust, for all we know. But I'll lay you twelve to
hree, citizens, seeing as how they come from a plane-
ary alliance that's founded on magic and not science
. . . I'll lay you twelve to three they feed and grow fat
on the plain scared-sick terror that's coming off this
planet like a hurricane. I'll just *bet* you they do!"

The Grannys looked at each other, and back at Charity's confident face on the comset screen. She could be
right; she'd always had an uncanny way of knowing
things, made up of three parts common sense, three
parts intuition, three parts blind luck, and one part they
didn't care to put a name to.

"It is just possible," Charity went on, "that if we
can't stop them we can at least slow them down some.
If we can only be calm, and leave off feeding them fear,
while we think what to do. It can't hurt, and it might
help. I want you to turn your hand to something else
than being scared, you hear me? Times tables, that's
always good. Or counting backwards from one hundred
by threes, that's even better. You can't keep your mind
on being scared if you're doing that. You tadlings as
don't have your numbers mastered, or anybody as is so
scared they've *lost* their numbers, you do the alphabet
backwards. *Back*wards, now! You can't do that and give
off terror at the same time."

The people listening agreed that it made sense, and
even if it hadn't it would be something to do; and those
that had no comsets any longer had neighbors pounding
on their doors to tell them.

Charity's voice went on and on, soothing and stroking, going out to four Kingdoms. Even Veritas Truebreed Motley, nursing his aching temples with a cold cloth at Brightwater, was nodding agreement. She had the principle right, however ignorant she might be of its workings.

"Now," said Charity of Airy, "I'll do it with you. We'll all be calm together, calm as pond water. 100. 97. 94. 91. Hmmmm . . . 88 . . . 85 . . ."

In the houses, they said it with her. And the tadlings tried the other thing and were amazed at how hard it was. Glottal stop, that was easy. Z, to go on with. Y, and then X, a person could manage. But from there on it was hard work, and who ever would of thought it? The alphabet, that everybody knew like they knew the look of their thumbs! Backwards it fairly brought the sweat out all over you. X . . . Q?

"Can't be Q!" said a tiny one, crossly, stamping her foot. "It's not time yet for Q!"

"What is it, then?" challenged her brother. "You're so smart . . . oh! I know! W! Before X comes W!"

"Pheeyeew," fussed the little girl. "W . . . now, let's us just see . . ."

Charity of Airy and the Grannys were well satisfied; they could feel the easing in the air almost immediately. It was just as well, under the circumstances, that none of them could see or sense the carnage in Smith Kingdom, where Lincoln Parradyne Smith the 39th was paying the penalty for his phony Granny that *was* no Granny, and the people of the Kingdom along with him. Long before it occurred to any of the other Magicians of Rank to ask a Mule to pass the message along to

149

the Mules of Smith, Lincoln Parradyne had paid his bill in full; he lay dead on the floor of the Throne Room, his brain crisped in his skull like a dead coal. And the only thing spared him was the horror outside and in, where the people of Smith trampled one another in their panic as they tried insanely to flee the menace above them. The crystal over Castle Smith was just a little different; its color matched the color of the blood smeared on the streets and the stairs of the town, almost exactly.

Troublesome of Brightwater lifted her sister out of the spring and held her close, sacred water and all, wondering if she had ever been so happy before. Bring on the giant alien crystals, bring on the slimy alien wickednesses, bring on anything you fancied; nevertheless, her sister was awake again.

Responsible fought herself free of Troublesome's embrace, which was somewhat more enthusiastic than was compatible with breathing.

"Troublesome?"

She tugged at the long black braid, to get Troublesome's attention, and wiped some of the water off her face, and asked plaintively if she could *please* have an explanation. It was not every day a person woke up naked in a creek, with a crowd attending.

She listened, her face growing more and more stern, while she was told. All about the awfulness that had come when she was put in pseudocoma. The poverty and the sickness and the weather all uncontrolled . . . it sounded like the tales of Old Earth . . . and nobody knowing what might be happening anyplace but the four Kingdoms of the Alliance, except for rumors. All about the Grannys' climb up the mountain, and Troublesome's dreadful ocean voyage. And when the part about Lewis Motley Wommack the 33rd came along, she cried out a broad word in total indignation that startled Silverweb of McDaniels right out of the last scraps of her rapture.

"It would of been when I was asleep, Troublesome!" declared Responsible of Brightwater. "That fool man! Ignorant, that's what he is, not to mention no sense at all. Half the night on Brightwater it's day on Kintucky, clear across that ocean on the other side of the world—did he never learn *anything*? I was dreaming . . . I remember the dreams. Oh, I remember them well, and they're not fit for Silverweb's ears. But never, never did I imagine that while I dreamed I was intruding on his mind. . . . The *id*iot! Oh, I'll make him pay, I promise you—oh, how I'll make him pay! He'll curse the day he was born, and long for the day that death releases him before I'm through . . . *stup*id man!"

"He is that," said Troublesome. "He might have asked you—but he wouldn't stoop. That's how he put it."

Responsible struggled from her sister's arms onto the rocks, where she sat hugging her knees and clothed only in her long hair, that was almost dry now in the hot desert sun.

"It was the Timecorner Prophecy," she said sorrowfully, "and no way to escape it. But I must say there's nothing elegant to the way it was fulfilled."

"Nor any excuse," said Silverweb. "For either him *or* you."

Responsible hadn't any interest at that moment in subtle moral questions. "*Now* what?" she said. She was a tad dazed, but she was not so addled that she intended to get into a discussion of how she and young Wommack might have managed to avoid what had been decreed since the beginning of time. What she wanted to know was the status of things.

Before Troublesome or Silverweb could speak, the Skerrys took it up.

RESPONSIBLE OF BRIGHTWATER, THE PLANETS OF THE GARNET RING NOW SEE THIS WORLD AS RIPE FOR THE CONQUERING, AND THEY HAVE COME TO PLUCK IT—IT FALLS NOW WITHIN THEIR LAWS OF COLONIAL RIGHT.

I CAN SEE THAT IT MIGHT, Responsible replied, not caring how much her mindspeaking might startle the other two women. There didn't seem to be much left in the way of secrets anyhow. WHAT HAVE THEY DONE, EXACTLY?

THEY HAVE HEARD THE REPORT OF THE OUT-CABAL, THAT THIS WORLD HAS FALLEN TO ANARCHY AND DISAS-TERS, AND THEY HAVE SET A . . . YOU HAVE NO SEMANTIC CONSTRUCT FOR IT. NO . . . YOU DO! YOU MUST IMAGINE A STORAGE CELL, DAUGHTER OF BRIGHTWATER, ONE HUNDRED AND TEN FEET FROM POINT TO POINT, POISED OVER EACH AND EVERY OZARK CASTLE AND FEEDING NOW —CHARGING NOW—WHILE WE STAND HERE TALKING. THEY ARE SHAPED LIKE DIAMONDS, AND YOU WOULD CALL THEM . . . CRYSTALS. THEY ARE DEADLY, AND THERE IS VERY LITTLE TIME.

WHAT HAS BEEN DONE? Responsible asked them, and
Troublesome realized suddenly that her sister's mind-
voice was just that, a voice, and not bells. When she had
the leisure, *if* she had the leisure, she would consider the
question of why that caused no barrier to the conversation. HAVE THEY BROUGHT OUT THE LASERS AGAINST
THE THINGS? HAVE THEY TRIED A TRANSFORMATION, A
DELETION TRANSFORMATION WITH ALL THE NINE MAGI-
CIANS OF RANK—

The Skerry cut her off.

YOU FORGET, it said. THERE HAS BEEN NO MAGIC ON
THIS WORLD WHILE YOU SLEPT—YOU HAVE BORNE IT ALL
WITHIN YOUR SELF. AS FOR THE LASERS, YOUR PEOPLE
HAVE NO WAY OF KNOWING WHAT IT MIGHT DO IF THEY
WERE TO PIERCE THE CRYSTALS, OR EVEN IF THEY WERE
TO TRY—NOR DO WE, NOR DO THE MULES, NOR DO THE
GENTLES. THE GENTLES, DAUGHTER OF BRIGHTWATER,
ARE VERY DISTRESSED BY ALL THIS. . . . I DO NOT
KNOW IF THEY WILL EVER COME UP TO THE DAYLIGHT
AGAIN. NOW, WE ALL ASK THE SAME THING, AND IT SEEMS
TO US ONLY JUSTICE, SINCE IT IS YOUR PEOPLE WHO
HAVE BROUGHT ALL THIS UPON US. WE ASK THAT YOU
DO SOMETHING, FOR THIS WORLD IS IN YOUR CHARGE.

It seemed to Troublesome that that wasn't justice at
all, or even likely, and she and Silverweb both protested
at once that Responsible was bound to be weak and like
a newborn babe for some time, that she would have to
get her strength back as anybody does after a long time
ill, and that asking her to take on a whole passel of alien
planets in her condition was downright ridiculous. It
came out garbled, a scrap from Troublesome and a scrap

from Silverweb, and some scraps from both, but they were of one mind on the matter.

What they had not taken into account was the strength of the energy that was being lent to Responsible by the Skerrys and the Mules. This was their planet, too, and had been theirs many thousands of years before ever an Ozarker set foot on it, and they had no desire to see it fall to the Garnet Ring, with who knew what consequences to follow. They didn't know a great deal about the peoples of the Garnet Ring, but they knew enough to be sure they weren't anybody you'd want for neighbors, and never mind the details.

Responsible of Brightwater gave her sister and Silverweb one look of considerable irritation, drew on the more than ample reservoir of energy the Mules and the Skerrys were offering her, and before the other two women could so much as draw a breath she had SNAPPED the three of them back to her own bedroom at Castle Brightwater, leaving Sterling to bring the wagon home.

Sitting on the edge of her bed, where she'd lain so long silent and motionless, she clucked her tongue, and glared at Troublesome and Silverweb, both of them more than slightly startled by their unaccustomed mode of transportation.

"This won't do," announced Responsible. "This won't do at all. Let me get something on my bones besides my skin, and I'll see to it."

And she headed for her wardrobe with her hands already busy braiding her hair, pausing only the few seconds it took to advise Troublesome that she'd never *seen* anybody quite so grubby and it would be a good thing if she had a tidy-up before she forgot how the parts of a decent female were supposed to be arranged.

# CHAPTER 10

"My lady—I am afraid."

The words came from an unusual source; Jessica of Lewis, Teacher Jessica these past seven months, was in the usual run of things a tower of strength. She was a true Three: brilliant, creative, high-spirited, and one for whom everything seemed to come easily. She had slipped into the Teaching Order as a hand slips into a glove made to its measure. None of the usual kicking at the traces for Jessica of Lewis. Not a flicker when her beloved books—"*Real* books!" the others had whispered. "Not micros, *real* books! And three of them!"— had been taken from her and added to the community library in Castle Wommack's north wing. When all the rest were down, it was Teacher Jessica they relied on, to bring their spirits up and to remind them once again that for those that are vowed to poverty the experience of poverty is no hardship.

Now she sat in Faculty Meeting, fifth down from Teacher Jewel of Wommack, so fast had she ascended through the ranks, and said: "My lady, I am afraid."

"We are all afraid," Teacher Jewel responded. "Not to be afraid would show a lack of common sense, or an unhealthy detachment from reality. There is a group consensus; nowhere in that consensus is there space for the crystal suspended above this Castle. How could we *not* be afraid?"

"That bodacious great rock hanging over our heads and ready for to drip down blood, it looks like . . . Law! Teacher Jessica, I should *hope* we're afraid!"

"If it is a rock," said Jewel of Wommack carefully, giving the new Teacher Candidate a measuring look, "what is holding it where it is, Cousin Naomi? Rocks do not float, neither do they fly. And there is no more magic."

Naomi of Wommack met her kinswoman's eyes without flinching; a good sign, thought Jewel. Naomi's speech was rougher than any Candidate's they had accepted yet; one would have thought she was trying for the formspeech used by the Grannys, except that even the Grannys no longer said "for to" before their verbs . . . perhaps in a moment of great excitement one might, but Jewel could not recall an example. Naomi had come out of a pocket on the far side of the Wilderness Lands of Kintucky, from a cluster of six households so isolated they had not had comsets even before Responsible of Brightwater was struck down. The rest of Kintucky had not even known they were there, and given the possibilities of marriage open to them they would not have lasted long—it was good fortune a Teacher, canvassing the Wilderness on her Mule, had stumbled across them.

"There will be again," said Naomi, confident as a child. "As there do be star and sun and tree. Somehow it's got a hitch in it, it's a kind of drought as comes in a bad year for the rains, but no reason for to doubt. *I don't doubt.*"

Jewel of Wommack believed her; she was as transparent as thin new ice on a puddle. And—always provided they all lived through whatever this crisis was—Naomi's ways might require more polishing than the other Candidates' had. *Maybe.* Jewel had discussed it when Naomi of Wommack joined them, and there had been disagreement among the senior faculty.

"She will be going back to Teach in the Wilderness Lands and along their borders," Jewel had reminded them. "Might could be that if her speech and her manners are greatly changed they won't trust her there, and trust is the foundation of Teaching. Think of my brother—when he took up the speechmode of the Magicians of Rank, purely to spite them, and then kept it up purely to spite the *rest* of us—think how it changed the way people behaved around him. He has a good deal more difficulty coaxing the young women into the haymows than he had when he spoke like anybody else . . . and a very good thing that is, I might add."

"But how, my lady," the others had protested, letting the matter of Lewis Motley drop, "how can she be respected if she speaks like she does, and drinks her coffee out of her saucer?"

Jewel's eyes, always dark blue, had gone even darker, and she had rebuked them sharply, reminding them for what seemed to her the ten thousandth time that it was *presence* that inspired respect, not fine manners and flowery speech.

"Do you ever look at your Teachers' Manuals?" she had asked them, exasperated. "It's set down there for you clearly enough, if you'd only look!"

It was among the Rules Major:

> The essence of inspiring belief is to achieve *congruence*, so that the channel of the voice and the channel of the body are in every smallest feature in true harmony.

And the codicil:

> And it would be well if the channel of the heart could be harmonious as well, providing always for the protection of the innocent.

That is . . . if you knew too much, keep it to yourself, and never mind the congruence of the heart, which was why it went in a codicil.

Candidate Naomi of Wommack met the congruence requirement to perfection. Her words were rough, her features were rough, her manners were rough, her movements were rough. She strode when she walked, she leaped up when she stood, she collapsed in a heap when she sat. . . .

"It is congruence," Teacher Jewel had said, ending the discussion. "It may be of great value. I know no requirement that Teachers must be like dolls, all matched the way the Grannys are. I may in fact go back to an easier way of speaking my own self; I was more comfortable that way."

A voice in the back of her head had said sadly: *No, you will not.* And she had known it was true. Senior

Teacher of the Order, and not yet sixteen—she needed every mark of authority she could get, including the elegant speechmode—not quite his own, but elegant nonetheless—in which Lewis Motley Wommack had drilled her till she wept. He had been quite right.

"My lady?"

Jewel was wrenched from her reverie, and embarrassed that she'd been able to fall into it, considering the circumstances.

"I apologize," she said distractedly. "My mind was somewhere . . . in a pleasanter time."

"We are wondering," said the speaker, a young Teacher whose voice had the granite edge fright gives when held back on tight rein, "if we should go on with the lessons today. We are afraid . . . the children are even more so."

"And what are the children doing at this moment, Teacher Cristabel?" Jewel asked her. "Do you know?"

"Huddled around their parents, sitting in their laps and being rocked if they're little enough, cowering under beds and porches . . . anything to get out of sight of that . . . thing. Whatever it is."

"In that case," said Jewel of Wommack resolutely, "we will of course go on with lessons. And the quicker the better. The most helpful thing we could do would be to present those children with the idea that there is order in their days *despite* that unholy object, and that it hasn't the power to make the grownups set aside the usual daily routine."

One of her faculty had a thought that had been thick on the far side of the world, in Airy Kingdom.

"They are all about to die," she said. "Better they die together than apart."

Jewel felt a rage that would be no help here, and she put it aside to be dealt with another time, and set her questions.

"Teacher Cecilia," she asked, "how is it that you know they, or any of us, are about to die?"

"My lady!"

"Well? If you have information, speak up; and if you have none, hold your peace. Has that crystal done any one of us, or any thing, injury?"

"Not yet, my lady."

"Not yet! But it will, eh? It does not fit the group consensus, will not be poked or shoved into the model we have built and labeled HERE SITS THE REAL WORLD . . . and *therefore*, it has to be a source of death."

"But my lady—"

"Per*haps*," said Jewel icily, "might could be the time has come for a change in that model. Had you thought of that? It is unknown; one fears the unknown. No doubt the first rainbow ever to be seen in the sky had people running and squalling, too."

Teacher Candidate Naomi was fascinated, Jewel could tell, and before she could call out something disgraceful, the Senior Teacher moved smoothly on into her next sentence.

"Until such time as we have evidence that that thing is a danger, we will behave normally," she instructed them. "That is our duty."

The Teachers and the Candidates nodded, though some did it reluctantly. They could see the rightness of what she said, and hoped those Teachers out riding their circuits or in residence in small towns beyond reach of the Castle would see it as well. The sight of the Teachers at their posts presenting history and grammar and mathematics and ecology and music theory to the children, as they did on any other day, would go a long way toward calming any panic. Business as usual, that was what was needed.

Lewis Motley Wommack the 33rd must have thought so, too. He came into the room in a fury, demanding to know why they weren't already on their way to their classes.

Jewel's voice sliced the air like a whip: "When *I* say that they are to go to their classes, they will go—and not until!"

The other women dropped their eyes and folded their hands; except for Naomi, who would not for anything have missed a single detail of the confrontation between brother and sister.

"Jewel, I do not mean to interfere—" the young man began.

"Then don't. Go on about your business . . . if you have any business . . . and leave us to ours. You have nothing to contribute here, and we have no time to coddle you."

*I will never stop paying,* thought Lewis Motley; *never. She wanted a home, and a man's body beside hers at night, and babes in her arms, and tadlings playing round her that looked just like that man; that's all she ever wanted. And I gave her this instead.*

163

It had been necessary, he was still convinced of that. Without the comsets, cut off from the rest of the continents, the people of Kintucky would have been condemned to ignorance and superstition; the Teachers had been absolutely necessary. But she was not going to forgive him.

And there'd been the matter of Responsible of Brightwater . . . that had *not* been necessary.

He gave her a stiff and formal nod, longing for the days when she'd worshiped the ground he walked on and the air he breathed. He wondered sometimes if he would ever love anything or anyone as he loved his little sister. He hoped not.

"I beg your pardon," said the former Guardian of Castle Wommack, and closed the door quietly behind him as he made his exit.

"Now then," said Jewel—and they all understood; the incident had not happened—"the only question is what you are to tell the children. And we must decide quickly, because you should be in your classrooms in ten minutes, and well prepared. Suggestions, please."

Teacher Sharon of Airy, second in rank to Jewel herself, spoke first.

"Do we *know* anything?"

"Nothing," said Jewel. "It was not there; it appeared out of nowhere and it *was* there; it remains there. It grows darker in color, and the Castle throbs with the vibration it is emitting. That is all."

"We cannot tell the children that!"

"Why not? It is the truth."

# And Then There'll Be Fireworks

The protests came from every one of the seventeen who sat around the table, except Naomi of Wommack.

"Dozens," said Naomi. "What point is there making up tales and pretty lies? Reckon any tadling smart enough to do his three-times is going to see we're lying —they do, you know. You can't lie to tadlings. Best they see we know what they know and *howsomever*, pointy rock or no pointy rock, we're there for to teach same as always. *Unless* one of youall has an explanation to offer 'em as will pass for truth."

"Well? Have you?" Jewel asked the silent women.

"It seems harsh," said Teacher Sharon, considering.

"It is quite clear," Jewel of Wommack told her hesitant faculty, "that whatever that is up there, it was not brought us by the Good Fairies for our delight. What is harsh is letting those children cower and shiver and cry all the day long while we sit here and console one another. You will go to your classes—as usual. If the children ask what that is in the air, you will say you don't know, and you will go on with your lessons—as usual. If they do not bring it up, *you* will not bring it up. As for me, I will get the fastest Mule we have in the stables and ride out to try to reach the Teachers in the country schools, as many as I can, and I will be telling them what I have told you. As usual. Do youall understand?"

"Yes, my lady."

Fifteen grudging yes-my-ladys, and one willing one from Naomi of Wommack; Naomi would of been willing, Jewel suspected, if ordered to lay herself full length in a fire.

165

"Let's get on with it, then," said Teacher Jewel, and she took up the small bell at her right hand to give the three rings of dismissal.

So it was that Jewel of Wommack was not in Booneville when the emergency alarms shrilled from every comset in the Castle and the town. She was out on Gamaliel, a Mule short in temper but long on endurance, making her way around a thicket of tangled briars toward the thirty-one families of Capertown, six miles beyond the borders of the capital.

There was a delay while the people realized what the sound was, it had been so long. For a few moments they thought it was something new from the horror in the sky, and the Teachers were hard put to it to keep their charges calm as they waited for word to come explaining it to *them*. They kept their voices steady and went on with the measured presentation of principles and concepts, and if their hands trembled they clasped them firmly behind their backs. The astonishing noise went on and on and on. And then, almost everywhere at once, people remembered.

"It's the comset alarm!" It came from a hundred places. People stared at one another, and shouted: "What does it mean?"

The comsets had been silent on Kintucky two years at least; and even when they'd been an ever present part of daily life, the *alarm* had been rare. It was no wonder they were confused. But when they turned to look at the comset screens set in their housewalls they saw that it was true; they were functioning again. The red call light

166

in the upper right-hand corner of each screen was blinking steadily on and off, and the alarm shrilled on. Those that had hung a picture or a weaving over the screen to escape its dead gray eye always staring at them rushed to take away the barrier and get to the ON stud.

"Ah, the Holy One be praised, the Holy One be praised!" cried Granny Copperdell at Castle Wommack. "*Will* you look? It's herself, oh glory be, it's herself! It's Responsible of Brightwater her*self!*"

First a miracle of terror, now a miracle of some other kind . . . life was confusing. But even in the classrooms everything else stopped, while the people of Ozark listened to Responsible's voice.

She began by explaining, for those Castles that might not yet know, what the crystals were and where they came from. She spoke hurriedly and promised them details later, when there was more time.

"But for now," she said, "the details don't matter. For now, youall must listen to me, and pay close attention to what I say, and waste no more time in carry-ons. Listen, now!

"The peoples of the Garnet Ring are not savages— they have laws. By their laws they may move to conquer only planets and systems of planets that are governed, as they are, by magic rather than by science. And of *those* planets they are constrained to conquer only in two situations: first, when the planet they're hankering after has gone to anarchy and has no government of its own to be displaced; second, if the planet they fancy is dying anyway, of natural disasters or of war. Ozark—*this* planet— comes near meeting both those conditions at this very minute, if what I'm told is true; and I've no reason to doubt it. And that is why the Garnet Ring has set those crystals in our skies.

"I do not know what the crystals will do if they aren't stopped," she told them. "I haven't the least idea. I do know, however, that they have power enough to destroy us twelve times over, no matter how it is they go about it. And I know how to *stop* them! If youall will help me, and waste not one second."

Responsible paused and gave them time to take all that in, and beside her, beyond the range of the cameras, Troublesome squeezed her sister's left hand, and Silverweb of McDaniels held tightly to her right hand, and the Grannys sat with their hands pressed to their lips. As for Veritas Truebreed Motley, he paced. There was no way of knowing if the comsets were working on the other continents where they'd been disused all this time. There was no way of knowing if there was anybody left alive on some of those continents to hear the alarm and turn on the comsets if they *did* still work. And there was no way, for sure there was no way, to predict whether, even if everything was working and all the Ozarkers were hanging on Responsible's every word, she would be able to persuade them. The suspense was almost as hard on him as his humiliation. *How* had Responsible of Brightwater been brought out of pseudocoma, without the help of the Magicians of Rank? Nobody would tell him; Responsible had just smiled, a maddening gleeful smile, when he tried to find out.

Veritas Truebreed smacked his fist in his palm, and he paced.

Meanwhile, Responsible went on talking, keeping her voice in the mode that carried the message: THERE IS NO QUESTION BUT THAT I WILL BE OBEYED. "At every Castle," she said, "you will call a Family Meeting, and elect —at once!—a Delegate to the New Confederation of Continents of Ozark. The Magicians of Rank will SNAP the Delegates here to Brightwater as quickly as you choose them . . . if you have no Magician of Rank in residence, be ready; one will be with you within the next half hour, and will not be pleased if you have no Delegate ready to return with him when he arrives, I warn you. Confederation Hall is at this very minute being made ready for the Delegates—"

Troublesome whistled softly, long and low, and Silverweb smiled at the lie, and the two of them—followed by the Grannys at as much speed as the old women could muster—headed out of Castle Brightwater for Confederation Hall, with Troublesome waving the keys above her head to show she still had them.

"Once the Delegates are here," Responsible went on, "they will offer a motion that a New Confederation be formed, second it, and pass it by unanimous vote—they will have ample time and more than ample time to write a new Constitution and work out all the trimmings and doodads they care to, when the crystals have been withdrawn. But that *will not be enough.*

"It will be necessary," she told them solemnly, "to call the roll."

That had never been done within the memory of anyone living, nor the memory of their parents, nor their grandparents. Very early, before the Ozarkers had moved out from Marktwain and their number had been small, it had been done. But now?

"The Garnet Ring wants this planet very badly," said Responsible. "Whatever you have done to it as I slept, and I understand that you have not been idle in your destruction, it is still rich in ores and forests and land and seawater . . . everything that a crowded system like the Garnet Ring needs and does not have. They have set no controls on their population and no controls on their greed—they will not give us up for a gesture. It will be done, one vote at a time, for every citizen over the age of twelve years, Kingdom by Kingdom. Stay at your comsets, and when the Chair says to begin, you will answer one at a time, in an orderly fashion. You will say, for example: 'I, So-and-So of Clark, hereby cast my vote for the New Confederation, and I say *Aye*; let it be so recorded.' It is of course your privilege to vote *against* the New Confederation; if enough of you do so, we will learn what the Garnet Ring proposes to do with us."

And she let them think about *that* a while. As a democratic method of persuasion, it had its shortcomings, and she was conscious of them. On the other hand, death or slavery weren't overly democratic either, and they appeared to be the other alternatives. If the means turned out not to be justified by the ends, she would have some paying to do. She'd worry about that when it happened. Right now, she had a world to convince.

A comcrew tech stuck his head in at the door, then, and raised both fists above his head and shook them at her. That meant the data was back to the computers;

that meant the comsets had been turned on everywhere
—even on Tinaseeh. That meant they were working,
and it meant there were Ozarkers to watch them. Responsible would have jumped up and down for joy except that it would of introduced an element of confusion into her presentation.

She nodded at the man and then began again, since
there might of been those coming in just then from the
woods or the fields, or only just finding a house that still
had a comset in working order. And she went through it
all one more time. And when she got to the end of that,
she began *again*.

By the time she had reached the third recitation of
the manner of calling the roll of every Ozarker over the
age of twelve, the first Delegate had landed in the yard
of Confederation Hall, his arms clasped round the waist
of Shawn Merryweather Lewis the 7th, Magician of
Rank in residence at Castle Motley, the two of them
seated on a bedraggled and scrawny Mule without so
much as a saddle blanket. Never mind, though; it had
been able and willing—it had in fact been eager—to fly.

They were landing everywhere, and the Grannys of
Brightwater threw open the doors of Confederation
Hall and shouted them a welcome, while Troublesome
sneaked out the back door and went home, and Silverweb stood and smiled. Now they would show those
cursed Garnet Ringers, whatsoever they might be! They
would show them what a people united could do, how
swift and sure a freedom-loving people could move to
set up a new and a strong government, how quick such a

government could move to take care of such petty matters as weather and hunger and disease and disaster and war!

The Grannys were as near ecstasy as a Granny could get, and in the excitement of the moment they had not even noticed that the arthritis that had been crippling them was gone. They stood on the steps of Confederation Hall, holding the doors wide, the tears pouring down their faces, cheering as each new Delegate arrived, and as each Mule and Magician of Rank SNAPPED out of sight to go after the next one.

They paid no mind to the fact that Silverweb of McDaniels, amusement in her eyes and cobwebs on her dress, was headed back toward Castle Brightwater to see what she could do now to help Responsible. Nor did it occur to them that Troublesome was long gone.

It was a brand-new day.

# CHAPTER 11

On Tinaseeh there was no need for anybody to ride out
into the countryside to search out people beyond the
range of the comsets. The Castle stood grim and dark at
the central point of the three squares marked off by the
logs of ironwood, set upright side by side and lasered to
wicked points; this was Roebuck, capital city and only
settlement of Tinaseeh, and it had ample room within it
for the six hundred and three persons still alive in Traveller Kingdom.

Except for the members of the Family and the Magicians of Rank, except for the College of Deacons and
the Tutors—and except of course for Granny Leeward
—the people of Tinaseeh were frail and ill. Measles and
croup and hunger took the young; pneumonia and cancer and hunger took the old; and at the Castle the Magicians of Rank themselves took turns guarding the secret
stores of extra food and the priceless herbs. They could
trust nobody else with that duty.

When the comset alarms went off, piercing the
stillness that covered Roebuck like a visible miasma, broken only by the exhortations of Jeremiah Thomas Traveller the 26th and his Deacons—no child had laughed
on Tinaseeh in many days, and now they were past cry-
ing as well—they were like red-hot irons through the

ears of the silent people. And Jeremiah Thomas, knowing the high tone at once for what it had to be, cursed in a way that brought the members of his household upright in shock. They had never heard a single broad word cross his lips before, not one; and there he stood shaking his fist at the wall where the red comset light was blinking, and shouting fit to turn the air blue for miles around.

Granny Leeward was the first to recover, and the first to realize how little time they had.

"He's right," she said urgently, "though I'll not defend the filth he's used to express himself. . . . I do believe his mind's turned, and no wonder. But we should never of left the comsets in the houses! They ought to have been ripped out, made truly useless, the day we got back here from the accursed Grand Jubilee, aye, if not long before. Leaving them, that was a grave mistake, and Jeremiah Thomas is right thrice over! But listen—it will be a while, might could be quite a while—before the people remember what that sound is. Might could be they won't remember, for that matter; I don't recall they've ever heard it. *If* we hurry! *If* we get out and call them out of their houses before they notice the lights— those, now, they'll remember. All of you, you go fast, you go from house to house and silence the wicked things, cut the wires or whatever it is as makes them go, and we might could get out of this yet! If we hurry, mind!"

"What could it be for?" marveled Feebus Timothy Traveller the 6th, staring around at the others. "What do you suppose?"

"Whatever it is, it comes from the womb of evil," said Leeward viciously, "for only Brightwater has the means to send out that alarm. And whatever it is, we do not care to hear it!"

"Now, Granny Leeward," the young Magician of Rank protested, "it may have to do with the crystal! And if it does, we—"

"No doubt it *does* have to do with the crystal," Granny Leeward threw back at him. "And no doubt you're still not quite over that fever you came near taking, eh, Feebus Timothy? Of *course* it has to do with the crystal; and nevertheless, we do not choose to hear! Where is your *faith?*"

If the people of Tinaseeh had not been so weak and so sickly, the Family might have been able to bring it off. Some would of been in the half dozen stores of Roebuck; some in the schoolrooms of the Tutors; some outside the walls working in the forests or the fields; some would of been walking in the town on their way to or from any of these things. But far too many of the handful of people remaining were housebound by sickness, and from their pallets laid on cold bare floors they had demanded that the comsets be turned on, and they had heard every word spoken by Responsible of Brightwater.

While the rest of the Family and its deputies were racing through the streets to try to prevent that from happening, Granny Leeward and Jeremiah Thomas Traveller sat alone before the comset at Castle Traveller and heard it all—twice through. And when the others returned to report that they had failed, that they had been too late, the Granny was ready for them.

"Call the people together," she said. Her voice made them think of the water that ran deep in the Tinaseeh caves in utter blackness, too cold even for blindfish to survive. "Those as cannot walk are to be carried, and those as try to say you nay are to be offered . . . promised . . . a taste of the Long Whip. Everybody, every last chick and child, is to be brought into the Inner Courtyard to hear Jeremiah Thomas speak against this temptation. Souls are precious things—we'll not see them lost *this* easily!"

It took time, because the messengers were few and already tired from their first hasty dash through the town, but not so long as might have been expected, given the frail health of the people. The College of Deacons met some of them in the streets, already on their way, carrying sick children in their arms. And in not much more than an hour after the alarm had sounded, they were all assembled. The Family, the Magicians of Rank, the College of Deacons—they sat on a platform used in happier times for the feastday services of the church, meant to give space for the Reverends and the choirs. The people that could stand stood, lined up in a squared-off horseshoe with the platform at its open end. Those that couldn't manage that leaned against the rough walls or lay on their pallets on the ground, or were cradled in the arms of relatives and friends.

And Jeremiah Thomas Traveller spoke, while Granny Leeward sat at his right hand with the Long Whip coiled and ready in her lap, and a muscle twitching high in her right cheek just along the ridge of the bone.

"My people," said the Master of Castle Traveller tenderly, raising his arms and spreading them wide in the pastoral embrace, "you know how I love you! More dear to me you are than ever son or daughter was to other man, more tightly bound to me than ever the bonds of blood have been! For you are *the faithful* . . . out of holy suffering you have come pure and filled with precious, nay, with priceless grace; around you the wicked and the weak in spirit have fallen like grass before the scythe, and yet you have stood. *You* have not fallen. You have not shrunk from the blade, not from its very edge; when it was at your throat you have bent to give it the kiss of fearless love. You have never doubted! How I love you—perhaps I love you more even than is fitting, but the Holy One will forgive me that.

"And how do I know all this? How can I be sure? Oh, my beloved people, only think what has been vouchsafed to you this *glorious* day! Those the Almighty loves, those are chastened; those the Almighty trusts, *those* are tested; those the Holy One counts among the elect, those are sent the blessing of ultimate temptation that they may demonstrate their contempt for *all* temptation! And this has come to you, to *you*, to every last and least and weariest one of you . . . for the Almighty knows, knows in confident glory, that there *is no test* your faith is not equal to!

"When I think"—and here Jeremiah Thomas let his hands move in and cross over his heart, and he added a judicious quaver to his voice—"when I think what honor has been done you, my beloved flock, I am struck to the heart. Who am I, that this blessing should pour down on me? Who am I, that I should lead so mighty, so fearless, an army of souls? What an honor has been done *me*, the least of all the servants!

"Fall to your knees," urged Jeremiah Thomas Traveller the 26th, his words honey and oil spreading around him, "fall to your knees! The trollop has spoken again from the citadel of sin, and you have heard her! And unto you, beloved, has come the opportunity to say to the Daughter of Brightwater a *No!* that will echo throughout the farthest corners of this world! *No!* you will say, we are not afraid of the abomination that pulses and grows each moment more gorged with blood above our heads, for it is only one more of the puny tests sent to try our faith, and we *glory* in that trial! *No!* you will say, we are not afraid of your Garnet Ring, of your Out-Cabal, of your bedtime tales invented for the terrifying of little children—for we are not little children, but *warriors* of the faith! There is no Garnet Ring! There is no Out-Cabal! There are no alien peoples prepared to make of us slaves or victims! There is only the just symbol of the wrath of the Holy One Almighty, set in the skies above us as a sign of the anger we have earned . . . and when we cry out *No!* and *No!* and *No!* nine times nine times again to the Whore of Brightwater, that symbol will fade away as do the clouds, that bring the gentle rains, and as the sunlight, that makes way for the healing hours of the night!"

Beside him the Granny sat nodding, her face smooth

now with satisfaction, the Long Whip twitching every now and again at a particularly telling phrase from the lips of her son.

The "mighty army" listened in silence, and they heard the man out, as was proper. There were some that had been standing, and as the sentences rolled on slipped to the ground or leaned more heavily against the walls; but not one left, and not one made a sound.

And then, when the last Amen had been shouted out and Jeremiah Thomas Traveller stood soaked with sweat and glowing with his righteous exultation, and ordered them back to their homes to take a day's holiday for prayer, one man stepped forward. Eustace Laddercane Traveller the 4th, him that had had a wife and ten children, and had seen that wife die in the throes of giving that tenth child birth, and had seen five more of his tadlings harvested by death since the day he had stood and forced them to watch the public whipping of Avalon of Wommack. He stepped out from among the others and walked straight and without so much as a tremble to his lips right up to the platform. The Granny leaned forward, uneasy, though her son had dropped to *his* knees and was holding out his arms to gather in this man he thought overcome with the emotions of the moment; and the Granny was right in her judgment.

Eustace Laddercane Traveller looked them over where they held their places. The Master of Traveller, and his Family assembled, not a one lost to disease or privation. The four Magicians of Rank in their elegant black. The College of Deacons, all trim, to be sure, but all hearty, all with color in their cheeks. And when he'd looked them over one by one he turned his back on them, standing where the Long Whip could wrap him round without the Granny having to do more than raise her arm, and he called out in a voice as strong as Jeremiah Thomas's had been.

"The citadel of sin is just behind me," shouted Eustace Laddercane, "and its whore sits there holding the Long Whip and hovering over her loathsome son, him that is a *false* Reverend, and a false guardian, and the liar of all liars! Look at them . . . look well, for I've no skill at preaching, and I've got no words to sway you with—but I've got eyes, and so have you. *There* sits evil, and I know it when I see it. And if Granny Leeward does not strike me down, I will go as Delegate to the New Confederation at Brightwater, if I have to swim the Ocean of Storms and the Ocean of Remembrances to get there! And if she *does*, if she does—choose you another Delegate, and then go back to your homes and cast your votes for the only hope you have in this life or the next!" And he waited, then, only the set of his shoulders betraying his awareness of what might fall upon them in the seconds just ahead.

You would not have thought that dragtail pitiful crowd of people could manage to cheer or to shout or to clap their scrawny hands together, but you would of been wrong. Man, woman, and child, they roared their approval of Eustace Laddercane Traveller's words and of his election as Delegate, and the Inner Courtyard became a forest of fists, raised high and waving their defiance, now and forevermore. On the platform, the rats were abandoning ship: the Family was moving back, as far as they could get from the howling mob; the members of the College of Deacons were leaping from the platform into the crowd to join the revolt; and the Magicians of Rank were squabbling among themselves as to which should be the one to SNAP the Delegate to the meeting at Confederation Hall.

Only the Granny held fast, rocking slowly where she sat, letting the Long Whip fall from her nerveless hands in utter disgust. She knew they would not touch her. Not even the father of little Avalon of Wommack. And she knew it was not because they feared her, one old lady deserted now by everything that had made her powerful. It was because they would sooner have touched the most uncanny creature that ever lurked at the bottom of a fouled sea and dragged itself across the swollen bodies of things long dead to feed upon them. She would have many a long and lonely year to rock, and to remember . . . she was the youngest of all the Grannys.

The process of re-forming the central government of Ozark was an orderly one, despite the excitement. The Delegates filled the rows at the front, the Magicians of Rank found a space just behind them, and the Grannys that could get there filled the balcony. Delldon Mallard Smith the 2nd seized the occasion to tear off his purple and ermine robes and his crown and set them afire on the steps of the hall, causing a stink that permeated all the rest of the proceedings before the blaze could be put out; and he had some difficulty explaining the death of *his* Magician of Rank—justified for once, since in fact he did not understand why Lincoln Parradyne had died. But he was there, and though foolish he was willing.

The motion for a New Confederation was put forward, seconded, and carried; and the great roll called by comset, the voices coming in from all over Ozark.

Responsible of Brightwater, up in the balcony where she belonged, could have wept at the pitiful number of votes there were to cast. Ozark had had at least half a million people only two years ago; now, with every Kingdom heard from, and every citizen above twelve years shouting a hearty "Aye!", she could only fight back the tears . . . that number had been reduced to a fraction. It was going to be a long hard pull, rebuilding what had been so wantonly torn down and so casually destroyed, and it would be a very long time indeed before they need concern themselves again with controlling population growth. But she was not going to have any time for tears.

The Teaching Order on Kintucky, that was a good idea; she would be seeing that it spread far and had its branches in every Kingdom that would accept it. Missions of mercy were going to be needed, Magicians and Magicians of Rank, even the Grannys, flying in to feed the hungry and heal the sick and see what must be done to repair the devastation. Other missions, less open, their members very carefully chosen, must go to the Gentles, and to the Skerrys, and to the Mules; debts were owed, and they must be paid. The weather must be brought back under control, and the Magicians sent to hasten the process of regrowth over the wastelands that had been Arkansaw and Mizzurah . . . and if it were true, what she had been told, that the Masters of Castles Lewis and Motley were held hostage at Castle Farson, she would take pleasure in settling *that* score personally. Steps must be taken to work against the prejudice still smothering the Purdys, that the long feuds had only made deeper and more irrational. Something must be done to counter the mythology of the Wommack Curse, that had bloomed and fattened into a monstrous burden on the people that now put their faith in it . . . and that task she might could trust, with a little discreet assistance, to the Teachers of Wommack.

The three monarchies could put away their raggedy trappings now, and if the King of Castle Smith was any example to judge by, they'd be welcoming the opportunity to do so. She would send . . . yes, she would send Silverweb of McDaniels to supervise the long healing process on Tinaseeh, backed by the two Magicians of Rank that were Travellers by birth. High time the Farson brothers spread *their* talents around; with only eight Magicians of Rank left to serve the planet, they'd be needed. And high time Silverweb had something to do that would tie her to this earth a tad.

And there was the delicate problem of placating the Magicians of Rank. For them to know as much as they knew already was chancy and would interfere for a while with their effectiveness; for them to know anything more would destroy them utterly. She hadn't time to be everywhere and do everything herself, nor was that her role. Ways would have to be found, pretty fabrications that skirted the far edge of the truth, face-saving explanations that the eight distinguished gentlemen could grab at and cling to. That line of Veritas Truebreed's, that named her as a catalyst, would do for a start.

She leaned over the edge of the balcony, looking down on the back of the Delegation from Castle Wommack; it seemed to her that the shoulders of Lewis Motley Wommack the 33rd had lost a good deal of their arrogance. That suited her; and it would suit her to find him something exceptionally burdensome to do for all the rest of his life. Or until her anger was all used up, whichever just happened to come first.

She was still stunned at the lists, that seemed to be endless, of the dead and the injured and the desolate . . . that would be a pain she carried to her grave, she rather expected. But she could not afford to indulge it, as she could not afford to indulge herself in any other mercy granted the rest of the living creatures of this planet. Responsible of Brightwater, Meta-Magician of Ozark for this generation and young enough to have scores of long hard years ahead of her, watched only long enough to be certain that the one negative vote to come in on the roll call came from Granny Leeward of Castle Traveller. And then she stood up and stretched a tad, and headed back to her rooms to set to work.

Above the Castles of the Twelve Kingdoms of Ozark, slowly, reluctantly, the great crystals were going pale and silent. The thrumming that had filled the whole world for days was no more than a tone just at the limit of the ear's perception, and dying fast. In the stables, the Mules were whuffling their approval.

And Sterling waited, with a message for this Responsible, to be passed on when her death drew near to the next in line, and so on down through time:

THE OUT-CABAL REMINDS YOU THAT THE PLANET OZARK REMAINS UNDER CONSTANT OBSERVATION.

For information about joining the Ozark Offworld Auxiliary, the official organization for the Ozark Fantasy Trilogy, write to Suzette Haden Elgin, Route 4, Box 192-E, Huntsville, AR 72740. She'll be grateful if you send along a stamped self-addressed return envelope when you write.